TEHUATL

PATHFINDER PLAYERS' GUIDE

Author: Tom Knauss
Additional Design: Tim Hitchcock
Project Managers: Zach Glazar and Tom Knauss
Editor: Jeff Harkness
Pathfinder System Conversion: Michael "Mars" Russell
Art Direction: Casey Christofferson
Layout and Graphic Design: Charles A. Wright
Cover Design: Charle A. Wright
Cover Art: Colin Chan
Interior Art: Julio de Carvalho, Adrian Landeros, Santa Norvaisaite, Terry Pavlet, Thuan Pham, Hector Rodriguez, and Erica Willey
Cartography: Robert Altbauer

FROG GOD GAMES IS:

Bill Webb, Matthew J. Finch, Zach Glazar, Charles A. Wright, Edwin Nagy, Mike Badolato, John Barnhouse

FROG GOD GAMES
ISBN: 978-1-6656-0203-7

TABLE OF CONTENTS

Introduction

This product gives Pathfinder players and GM's spells, equipment, and magic items designed for the Tehuatl expansion to the World of the Lost Lands campaign setting. However, you are free to incorporate the resources contained within these pages to any section of the Lost Lands or any other world of your choosing.

Class Options

Adventurers generally begin their careers marching in lockstep along the same path followed by countless others before them. Regardless of whether they wield a weapon, channel potent arcane magic, or obtain the blessing of a deity or an ideology, the initial phase of their development rigidly adheres to a predetermined foundation of well-rounded skills and abilities designed to improve their chances of survival in a dangerous world. Yet, when adventurers amass a degree of basic training and experience under their belts, heroes ultimately diverge from their previously singular route and explore new roads teeming with exciting possibilities. Although these pathways are more specialized than the adventurer's previously generalized experience, the character's deviation from the norm proves versatile enough to allow the character to overcome any challenge standing in his or her way.

The class options already available to characters give them the tools to succeed in any environment, yet the residents of Tehuatl have also developed a diverse spectrum of alternative possibilities tailor made for the island's unique culture, religious beliefs, and political structure. Building upon centuries of traditions, equipment, and faith, as well as the harrowing demands of their tempestuous surroundings, the class options found in Tehuatl are more focused and customized than their traditionally universal counterparts. This chapter describes and details two options for each core character class. While they are specifically designed for characters adventuring in Tehuatl, they perform admirably in any other setting of your choosing.

Barbarian Archetypes

Civilization typically bestows the term barbarian onto anyone who lives outside its aegis and refuses to conform to the community's accepted standards. Some people even equate barbarians with wild animals, perceiving them as savage, untamed, amoral beasts aimlessly roaming across the wilderness. Despite the negative connotations, barbarians often emulate animals more than humanoids. Similar to their four-legged counterparts, barbarians live off the land rather than on it like sedentary people. They rarely put down permanent roots, preferring to constantly remain on the move, foraging for food and other necessities in the great outdoors. Unconstrained by society's rules and expectations, barbarians are free to fully tap into their emotions, giving them the power to channel their pent-up anger into a furious rage akin to a wild animal defending its young or a predatory beast charging toward its prey. Tehuatl's barbarians embody many of the preceding principles, though they also frequently interact with the fringes of civilization instead of dwelling far beyond its reach in relative isolation. Their contact with society is a conscious choice as well as a byproduct of the island's small size in comparison to the great continents of Akados and Libynos. Tehuatl's residents generally perceive barbarians as self-sufficient outsiders with a wicked mean streak.

Cuachicqueh

The elite Aztli warriors who follow this path abide by only one motto: Never take a backward step. Although classified as barbarians, those who follow the path of the cuachicqueh serve as a formal branch in most cities' military apparatuses. Known as the "shorn ones" in some circles, these utterly fearless soldiers shave their heads except for a long braid of hair over the left ear. They may also paint each half of their bald scalp a different color signifying their loyalty to a deity of their choosing or a political entity. These terrifying warriors stand at the vanguard of many armies where they use their colorful displays to showcase their bravery and wanton rage in a deliberate attempt to brutally crush and demoralize their frightened enemies. Barbarians adhering to this primal path exist across the island among the ranks of the Aztlis and the Poqozas.

Feathers. **(Su)** At 2nd level, feathers instantaneously sprout from your bald scalp while you rage, enhancing your courage and determination in battle. For the duration of your rage, you can take a move action as a swift action if the action moves you within five feet of an enemy. Being within five feet of an enemy when you start your move action does not fulfill the preceding requirement. In addition, you have a +2 bonus on attack rolls against hostile creatures leaving your reach and on saving throws against being frightened. If you use the Disengage action, your rage immediately ends. When the rage ends, the feathers instantly lose their magical properties and detach from your scalp. This ability replaces the rage power gained at 2nd level.

Plumage. **(Su)** At 4th level, you also control the coloration of your feathers from the Feathers class feature. Choose one of the following colors when you gain this ability. Your feathers also have the chosen effect. As a swift action, you may pluck one feather from your head and make a melee attack with the feather dealing 1d6 damage. The damage increases to 2d6 at 10th level, 3d6 at 15th level, and 4d6 at 20th level. You can make a melee attack with a detached feather only once per rage. The feather's color determines the damage type.

Black: Magical darkness fills a 10-foot-radius sphere around the black feathers. The darkness spreads around corners. The magical darkness immediately suppresses any nonmagical light source in the area. Creatures with darkvision cannot see through the darkness. Completely covering the feathers with an opaque object such as a helmet or a headdress blocks the darkness. If any of this area overlaps with an area of light created by a spell of 2nd level or lower, the spell that created the light is dispelled. A black feather deals cold damage.

Blue: Blue feathers give you a brief glimpse into the future. Roll two d20s and record one of the numbers you rolled. You can replace any attack roll or saving throw made by you with the recorded roll. You must choose to do so before the roll, and you can replace a roll in this way only once for the duration of your rage. A blue feather deals lightning damage.

Red: You gain resistance to fire damage equal to your level. A red feather deals fire damage.

Yellow: These feathers shine bright light in a 40-foot radius and dim light for an additional 40 feet. Completely covering the feathers with an opaque object such as a helmet or a headdress blocks the light. If any of this area overlaps with an area of darkness created by a spell of 2nd level or lower, the spell that created the darkness is dispelled. A yellow feather deals acid damage.

This ability replaces the rage power gained at 4th level.

Wondrous Plumage. **(Su)** At 6th level, choose one of the following colors when you gain this ability that you use when using the Feathers class feature. These feathers cannot be plucked from your scalp and used as a weapon.

Gray: These feathers create magical silence in a 20-foot-radius sphere that moves with you and spreads around corners. No sounds can be created within or pass through the sphere. Creatures entirely inside the sphere, including you, are deafened, immune to sonic damage, and cannot cast spells that require a verbal component.

Green: Your speed doubles, you gain a +2 bonus to AC, and you have a +2 on Reflex saving throws.

Orange: Your movement is unaffected by difficult terrain, and spells and other magical effects cannot reduce your speed, knock you prone, nor cause you to be restrained. You can spend five feet of movement to automatically escape nonmagical bonds such as manacles or a creature that has you grappled.

White: The first time you are subjected to an effect that would cause you to be paralyzed, petrified, or restrained during your rage, that effect is instead negated. Otherwise, you have a +2 on your saving throws against being paralyzed, petrified, or restrained.

This ability replaces the rage power gained at 6th level.

Two-Tone. **(Su)** Starting at 10th level, you can sprout both of feather colors from your Feathers class feature. You gain the effects of both colors at the same time. This ability replaces the rage power gained at 10th level.

No Retreat. **(Ex)** Starting at 14th level, opponents within range of your melee attacks who move out of your reach, even if they use the Disengage action to do so, must succeed on a CMB check against CMD or fall prone. If they fall prone, you can use an attack of opportunity to make a melee weapon attack against that creature. This ability replaces the rage power gained at 14th level.

Skin Flayer

The practice of flaying another creature's skin almost universally evokes fear and horror among humanoids. The residents of Tehuatl are no exception. Barbarians who follow this unusual path elicit wonderment and disgust from onlookers who seem simultaneously curious and disturbed by the grisly practice. Many Aztlis incorrectly mistake these barbarians for devotees of their god Zipe-Toteque. While some devotees may pay token homage to that deity, these fearsome warriors covet the skins of their fallen enemies for a purpose completely divested from making an offering to a disinterested god. They instead use their opponent's flesh to mimic the appearance of a vanquished foe or to emulate the traits of a defeated adversary. This path has recently gained significant traction among the island's goblinoid inhabitants in addition to its Aztli and Poqoza adherents.

Torn Flesh. **(Ex)** At 1st level, you can tear an opponent's flesh open with your melee weapon strikes. While you are raging, any creature other than an undead or a construct that you hit with a melee weapon dealing piercing or slashing damage must succeed on a Fortitude saving throw where the DC equals 10 + half your Barbarian level + your Constitution modifier or suffer bleed damage equal to one third your level (minimum one). This ability replaces fast movement and uncanny dodge.

Dig Deeper. **(Ex)** Beginning at 6th level, the sight of lacerated flesh feeds your anger. As a swift action while raging, you can make a melee attack against a creature other than an undead or a construct that you can see if the target was suffering from bleed damage at the start of the turn. You can use this ability only once per rage. This ability replaces the rage power gained at 6th level.

Wear the Flesh. **(Su)** At 10th level, you can ritualistically strip the flesh from a creature other than an undead or a construct, allowing you to use the dead creature's face as a mask. It takes one minute to remove the skin in this manner, regardless of the creature's size. You can perform the ritual only on a creature that died within the last hour. Anyone of the same size and creature type as the dead creature can wear the mask, giving that creature a +2 bonus on Disguise checks made to disguise themselves as the dead creature instead of the typical penalties.

The flesh mask falls apart one hour after the ritual's completion, rendering it useless. Once you use this feature to create a flesh mask, you cannot use it again for 24 hours. This ability replaces the rage power gained at 10th level.

Become the Beast. **(Su)** At 14th level, you can don a beast's skin, gaining its abilities and appearance. When you use this feature, you cast *beast shape IV* as a spell-like ability, though you must use the skin of a beast that died within the last hour as a material component. You must assume the form of the beast used as the spell's material component. You may only use this ability once per day. This ability replaces the rage power gained at 14th level and indomitable will.

Bard Archetypes

Humanoids express ideas, thoughts, and emotions through a variety of mediums. Words, music, dance, and art elicit a wide array of responses from the audience. Some stir the soul to anger, while others calm the savage beast. Those blessed with a flair for the dramatic or the rare gift of extraordinary insight into the human condition use these special talents to influence the actions of friend and foe alike. Bards take performance to an entirely new level. In their introspective eyes, the world is their canvas, a blank slate waiting for an artist to breathe life into a previously inanimate object. They can inspire others to achieve the impossible through their rousing performances or their repertoire of magical powers. While artistic expression may be seen as a luxury in some cultures, the people of Tehuatl consider these disciplines an essential part of the fabric of their lives.

Dance

Dancers never let choreographed movements impede their inspiration. The practitioners of this visual art frequently subscribe to the belief that forces greater than themselves direct their motions and steps for a nobler purpose than entertaining a crowd or wooing a prospective partner. The Dance, a loosely organized troupe of nomadic dancers wandering across Tehuatl, fervently subscribes to the preceding notion. Instead of conveying their art through formal classes or manuals, its members pass their secrets down from

generation to generation through oral tradition and trial and error. After years of practice, these bards affirmatively swear they can contact the underworld to channel the spirits of the dead into their rhythms. Indeed, those who observe them in action walk away with the same conviction.

Spirit Trance. **(Su)** At 1st level, you gain the ability to channel with the spirits of the dead as the Medium class abilities Spirit and Spirit Bonus with the following changes. You must select one spirit to channel when you gain this ability, this selection can not be changed. In addition, your séance only requires 15 minutes and can be done concurrently with regaining spell slots. This ability replaces bardic knowledge.

Ghost Drums. **(Su)** At 3rd level, if you perform on your drums for at least one minute, you can establish a link with the spirit world. Throughout your performance, you see glimpses of possible future events about to unfold. When your performance ends, you can use your swift action to perform one of the following activities: make a melee attack against a creature within five feet of you; cast a spell 2 or more levels lower than the highest level spells you can cast; or move up to half your speed. You can use this ability only once, and if you do not use it within one hour after completing your performance, its effects are wasted. The number of uses you have increase when you reach certain levels in this class. At 10th level, you have two uses, three uses at 15th level, and four uses at 20th level. This feature does not allow you to use more than one swift action per turn. You may only use this ability once per day. This ability replaces versatile performance.

Rhythms of the Drums. **(Su)** At 5th level, you can use your drums to aid you and allies. As a standard action, you can start a performance with your drums that lasts until the end of your next turn. During that time, you and any friendly creatures within 30 feet of you can move out of the reach of hostile creatures without provoking opportunity attacks from them. A creature must be able to hear you to gain this benefit. The performance ends early if you are incapacitated or silenced, or if you would voluntarily end it. At 7th level, you may perform this as a move action. At 13th level, you may perform this as a swift action. This ability replaces lore master.

Consult the Ghosts. (Su) At 10th level, you can consult the spirits for advice. If you perform for at least 10 minutes, you can open a link to the spirit world, allowing you to obtain guidance from otherworldly entities. Within one minute of completing your performance, you can ask a single question that can be answered with a yes or no response. You receive a correct answer to your question.

The spirits are not omniscient. The ghosts respond to the question based upon their knowledge. If the subject matter is outside their purview, such as asking what a deity is thinking or events on a distant planet, the spirits respond with an "uncertain" answer. A short phrase may be substituted for a one-word answer when deemed appropriate. If you fail to ask a question within the allotted time, you lose the opportunity to do so. You may use this ability once per day. This ability replaces jack of all trades.

FLOWER

For the people of Tehuatl, art and war walk hand in hand. Victory is often measured through visual achievements rather than tactical outcomes. Traditional armies assess the success or failure of a battle based upon territorial gains and enemy casualties. In Tehuatl, personal style and colorful imagery garner more attention in combat than brutal decapitations and gory beatings. Flower bards understand this principle better than all others. Flowers dazzle the eyes, nose, and skin. Their vibrant hues, tantalizing aromas, and velvety textures captivate the senses while they dance in the air and tumble down to earth. Newcomers to Tehuatl mistakenly view these easygoing bards as lazy, bohemian hedonists. Adventurers who make this foolish error sometimes pay with their lives.

Rain of Petals. (Su) At 3rd level, you can create a wondrous visual display. You can expend one use of your Bardic Performance to conjure hundreds of flower petals. The flower petals quickly float to the ground in a 10-foot-radius, 20-foot-high cylinder centered on a point you can see within 60 feet. Choose a number of creatures within the cylinder that you can see equal to or less than your Charisma modifier (minimum of one). Rain of petals affects only those creatures. The effects take place instantaneously and last until specified in each description. Choose one of the following flowers:

Marigold: Undead creatures within the cylinder must succeed on a Will saving throw where the DC equals 10 + half your Bard level + your Charisma modifier or take 2d4 positive energy damage. The damage increases when you reach certain levels in this class, increasing to 3d4 at 5th level, 4d4 at 10th level, and 5d4 at 15th level.

Dahlia: Creatures in the cylinder have a +2 on Reflex saving throws and may use a swift action to move their speed until the beginning of your next turn.

Orchid: Creatures in the cylinder must succeed on a Will saving throw where the DC equals 10 + half your Bard level + your Charisma modifier. On a failed saving throw, a creature cannot take a swift action, an attack of opportunity, or ready actions until the start of your next turn.

Yucca: Creatures in the cylinder who attempt a saving throw at the end of their turn against a magical spell or effect already in place may reroll any such saving throw until the beginning of your turn, taking the higher result.

This ability replaces inspire competence.

Swirling Bouquet. (Su) Starting at 3rd level, you may aid others attempting to avoid detection. When a creature you can see within 60 feet makes a Stealth check, you may use your immediate action to create a 10-foot-radius, 20-foot-high cylinder of swirling flowers centered on that creature. The swirling petals momentarily prevent other creatures from seeing the creature, giving it an opportunity to hide. Observers relying on sight suffer a -5 penalty on Perception checks made to detect the creature until the end of the hiding creature's turn. You may use this ability three times per day. This ability replaces well versed.

Plant Whisperer. (Su) At 6th level, you gain the limited ability to communicate and command plants. As a swift action, you can use *speak with plants* as a spell-like ability by expending one use of Bardic Performance, and flowers sprout from your skin. This ability replaces suggestion.

Flower Power. (Su) At 14th level, you create a mystical aroma capable of pacifying even the fiercest beasts. As a standard action, you magically conjure a potent, floral scent that only one creature of your choice within 30 feet of you can smell by expending two uses of Bardic Performance. The target must succeed on a Will saving throw where the DC equals 10 + half your Bard level + your Charisma modifier. Undead, constructs, and other creatures with no sense of smell automatically succeed on the saving throw. Creatures with the Scent suffer a -5 penalty on their saving throw.

On a failed saving throw, the target experiences a sense of peace and tranquility. The creature becomes so engrossed with the aroma that it ignores its surroundings. It suffers a -2 penalty on ability checks and saving throws and cannot take an Attack action, nor use spells or magical effects harmful to other creatures. At the end of each of its turns, the target can make another Will saving throw. On a success, the effect ends. The effect also ends if you or any of your companions do anything harmful to the target. This ability replaces frightening tune.

CLERIC ARCHETYPES

Beings imbued with immortality and omniscience can be a capricious and fickle lot. While worshippers may sometimes placate their angry moods with prayers and offerings, vain deities frequently demand more than a handful of unspoken pleas and bundles of trinkets. Gods exert their influence across entire worlds. In kind, they often expect their followers to reciprocate through grand demonstrations of supplication. Clerics, the gods' earthly intermediaries, lead these wondrous spectacles at the behest of their divine patrons. Many people view clerics as the divine being's worldly representative. However, their relationship with these distant entities is more complex than merely serving as their spokesperson. Although their chosen deity or belief system grants clerics the power to cast spells on their behalf, only a small handful of powerful priests directly communicate with their benefactor. Instead, clerics interpret their gods' intentions through signs, omens, and other events occurring around them. Based upon their observations, the cleric relies on his expertise and insight to either express his constituents' gratitude toward their merciful god or devise a plan to appease an irritated omnipotent being. Clerics and worshippers aspiring to curry favor from the gods of Tehuatl must often deal in extremes. The hero-gods who liberated the land from the emperor centuries earlier frequently demand sacrifices of goods and blood to keep the circle of life in motion.

NAGUAL

Throughout Tehuatl, elders speak in hushed whispers about men and women who can transform into beasts, giants, and other more exotic creatures. These legends refer to these deceitful shapeshifting beings as the nagual. Such creatures are especially reviled in Tehuatl because of their association with the disguised serpent advisors who served the island's former master, Emperor Tlatoani. The clerics subscribing to the tenets of this archetype believe it is their divine mission to root out and expose these imposters wherever they rear their ugly heads. In addition to unmasking the nagual, these clerics also learn to change their own forms and shapes to serve the needs of their deities. These clerics typically serve deities associated with shapeshifters or magic, such as Itztliteotl.

This archetype replaces channel energy.

Chant of Making. (Su) Starting at 1st level, you have a knack for preserving the integrity of magic items. When a magic item on your person would normally be destroyed or expend its final charge, you roll a d20. On a roll of 11 or higher, the magic item is not destroyed or the final charge is not expended. This feature does not protect magic items you voluntarily destroy or magic items normally destroyed after a single use, such as potions and scrolls.

True Form. (Su) Starting at 3rd level, you can force creatures to reassume their true form. As a standard action, you recite a ceremonial chant and momentarily close your eyes before reopening them. Each creature not in its true form within 30 feet, such as a shapechanger, a polymorphed creature, or a druid using its wild shape feature, must succeed on a Fortitude saving throw where the DC equals 10 + half your Cleric level + your Wisdom modifier or revert to its true form at the beginning of its next turn, using whatever action necessary to do so. It must then remain in its true form for one minute. True Form only affects creatures that have taken another physical form. Creatures wearing a mundane disguise or those using illusory magic to make them appear different are unaffected. You may use this ability a number of times per day equal to your Wisdom modifier.

Silvery Moon. (Su) Beginning at 5th level, you develop an affinity for silver, the bane of many shapeshifting creatures. As a standard action, you stretch your arms and emit moonlight equivalent to dim light that deals damage equal to five times your cleric level. The damage only affects creatures that have DR/silver, such as lycanthropes. Choose any of the preceding creatures you can see within 30 feet of you and divide the damage among them as you see fit. Creatures with vulnerability to silver take double damage from the feature. Silvery Moon deals no damage to all other creatures and affected creatures with total cover from you. The moonlight illuminates the area within 30 feet of you until the end of your turn. You may use this ability a number of times per day equal to your Wisdom modifier.

Amorphous. (Su) At 7th level, you gain the ability to temporarily transform into an ooze. As a swift action, you become amorphous until the end of your next turn. You retain your alignment, personality, hit points, and most ability scores, but your Dexterity score is reduced to the lower of your Dexterity score or 3. Your gear melds into your new form, though you cannot activate, use, wield, or otherwise benefit from any of your equipment. Likewise, you cannot speak, cast spells, or take any other action requiring hands or speech. Your speed slows to 10 feet, and you are immune to being blinded, deafened, or prone. You gain the Amorphous monster ability. You can move through a space as narrow as one inch wide without squeezing. You may use this ability a number of times per day equal to your Charisma modifier.

Ghostly Form. **(Su)** At 17th level, you develop a limited ability to move through creatures and objects. As a standard action, you transform into a wispy, translucent creature. Until the end of your next turn, you can move through other creatures and objects as if they were difficult terrain. You take 3d4 force damage if you end your turn inside an object. If you transform back into your true form while inside an object, you take 15d4 force damage at the beginning of each turn until you are freed. You may use this ability once per day.

TETZAUITL

For the superstitious people of Tehuatl, there are no coincidences. Instead, they see a divine hand behind most events, regardless of how mundane it may be. Portents, omens, and other signs lurk in the shadows, giving insight to those with the acuity to spot and interpret these hidden clues. Those individuals with the requisite wisdom to see and interpret these occurrences gain a significant upper hand against their adversaries as they acquire the ability to react quicker than those oblivious to what awaits them. Clerics from the Tetzauitl archetype hone their powers of perception to see the future. They and their followers typically venerate Nonotzali though they may also worship deities with an interest in prophecies or influencing the outcomes of forthcoming events.

Diminished Spellcasting. You receive one fewer spell slot at each spell level. When you get no spells per day at a spell level, you can cast domain spells of that level normally, but can only cast nondomain spells of that level if you get them as bonus spells. This ability alters the cleric's spellcasting.

Deja Vu. **(Su)** Perception becomes a class skill for you. In addition, whenever you roll a Perception check roll twice and take the better result. This ability alters class skills.

See Fate. **(Su)** Starting at 2nd level, you can expend one use of your Channel Energy to see potential outcomes for future events. As a standard action you observe your surroundings for signs and portents hidden to all others, allowing you to better anticipate the actions of other creatures. Each hostile creature within 30 feet of you must succeed on a Will saving throw against your Channel Energy DC. On a failed Will saving throw, the hostile creature suffers a -5 on Stealth checks, and it must succeed on a Reflex saving throw against your Channel Energy DC each time it uses an Attack of Opportunity. On a failed Reflex saving throw, the target's Attack of Opportunity is lost instead. The effect lasts for one minute.

Improve Fate. **(Su)** At 6th level, when a creature you can see within 30 feet of you makes a saving throw, you can use your immediate action to grant that creature a bonus to the roll equal to the number of dice your would roll for Channel Energy, expending one use of your Channel Energy. You make this choice after you see the roll, but before finding out whether the saving throw succeeds or fails.

Saw That Coming. **(Su)** At 8th level, you can use your Attack of Opportunity to partially block a blow when you are hit by a melee weapon attack. When you do so, the damage you take from the attack is reduced by your cleric level. You can use this feature a number of times per day equal to your Wisdom modifier.

Anticipate. **(Su)** At 17th level, whenever you roll a Reflex saving throw roll twice and take the better result. If you are not surprised, you also have roll twice and take the better result on initiative rolls.

DRUID ARCHETYPES

Nature may not be sentient, but it seems to have a mind of its own. Every attempt to control, predict, or tame nature ultimately fails. Cognizant of this inescapable reality, some intrepid souls opt down the path of understanding and coexisting with the great outdoors rather than endeavoring in the folly of subjugating it to their will. Druids treat nature as a valuable yet unpredictable ally instead of a staunch adversary. They walk alongside its wild beasts, tend to the vegetation around them, and exert limited authority over the weather and other calamitous events. These adventurers learn to assume the form of other creatures and wield magic to conjure creatures to aid them in their cause. Civilized people often view these wardens of the wilderness as isolationists. Indeed, druids are more devoted to maintaining nature's sanctity and advancing the interests of their chosen deity than to interacting with humanoid communities. Despite their independent leanings, druids belong to druidic circles made up of likeminded individuals devoted to expanding their knowledge of nature and defending their land against exploitation. Traditional druidic circles imported from other lands have gained some traction in Tehuatl, yet the island still maintains its own cadre of secretive organizations in isolated regions across the island. These groups focus their attention on preserving the integrity of a small area or championing the cause of an obscure deity with a limited domain.

FAULT

Tehuatl is a rocky, volatile island. The seismic forces deep beneath the ground shaped a land dominated by formidable peaks and scabrous crags. Indeed, the molten rock and ash forced to the surface countless years ago kept Tehuatl's proverbial head above the water when the great cataclysm washed away numerous adjacent lands. The Tepepan Mountains in the island's heart serve as a constant reminder of Tehuatl's fiery origins. Although these stony outposts seem lifeless, a band of druids known as the Circle of the Fault find inspiration among these cracks in the earth, most notably in the areas containing active volcanoes and fault lines. Firebrand dwarves make up a significant percentage of the circle's membership complemented by a smattering of other humanoid races. When the earth rumbles or a mountain spews hot gases into the air, these druids frequently gather at the impacted site to study the phenomenon and beseech the gods to end the calamity.

Firestarter. **(Sp)** At 1st level, you gain the Basic Pyrokinesis Kineticist utility talent. This ability replaces wild empathy.

Volcanic Stones. **(Sp)** Starting at 1st level, you gain the Kinetic Blast class ability and the Fire Blast wild talent from Kineticist. This ability replaces nature bond.

Volcano Walker. **(Ex)** At 6th level, you gain resistance to fire damage equal to your Druid level and immunity to poison damage from toxic gases. You may move through any sort of rocks or stones that are magically created or manipulated to impede movement, such as those created by *spike growth* at your normal speed and without taking damage or suffering any other impairment. This ability replaces woodland stride.

Progeny of Fire and Stone. **(Su)** Beginning at 9th level, you can bolster the might of elementals under your aegis. When a fire elemental or earth elemental you summoned or called ends its turn within five feet of you, that creature regains a number of hit points equal to half your druid level. In addition, you can use a standard action to touch one of the preceding creatures to grant that creature a +2 on attack rolls until the beginning of your next turn. This ability replaces venom immunity.

Tremor. **(Su)** At 15th level, you can cause a minor tremor. As a standard action, you create a seismic disturbance at a point on the ground that you can see within 500 feet of you. The tremor lasts for one minute. For the duration, the ground shakes in a 100-foot-radius circle centered on that point, rattling creatures and structures in contact with the ground in that area. The ground in the area becomes difficult terrain. Each creature on the ground that is doing an activity that requires concentration must succeed on a Concentration check every round. On a failed check, the creature's concentration is broken.

Each creature on the ground in the area must succeed on a Reflex saving throw where the DC is 10 + half your Druid level + your Constitution modifier at the end of each of your turns. On a failed Reflex saving throw, the creature is knocked prone. The tremor lacks the strength to damage soundly built permanent structures made from wood, stone, and other solid materials. The tremor deals 20 bludgeoning damage to any temporary or unsound permanent structures in contact with the ground at the start of your turn until the tremor ends. If a structure drops to 0 hit points, it collapses and potentially damages nearby creatures. A creature within half the distance of a structure's height must succeed on a Reflex saving throw where the DC is 10 + half your Druid level + your Constitution modifier to escape the collapse. On a failed saving throw, the creature is knocked prone and is buried under the debris. In addition, the falling debris deals bludgeoning damage to creatures buried beneath it. Stone, concrete, and other hard materials deal 5d6 bludgeoning damage. Wood and similar materials deal 3d6 bludgeoning damage, while leather, thatch, and other pliable materials deal 1d6 bludgeoning damage. Creatures buried beneath stone and rock must succeed on a DC 20 Escape Artist check to escape. Those beneath wood and similar materials must succeed on a DC 15 Escape Artist check, while those under leather and similar materials must succeed on a DC 10 Escape Artist check.

You may use this ability once per day. This ability replaces timeless body.

Maize

In Tehuatl, one food staple outshines all others — maize. Civilization would almost certainly falter without this cereal grain. Typically grown on cultivated land rather than harvested in the wild, maize plants can produce enough food to nourish vast populations of men and beasts, whether they are eaten in their immature state, ground into cornmeal, or dried for later consumption. The druids who make up the Circle of Maize recognize this inescapable fact of life. Despite its versatility, maize is a delicate crop susceptible to drought, fierce winds, pests, and other environmental hazards. To defend the plant against its enemies, the druids entrusted with its care form a virtually symbiotic bond with maize, allowing them to artificially grow kernels in their outstretched hands or to travel from one plant to another.

One with Maize. (Su) Starting at 2nd level, you can use a standard action to grow a small, magical ear of maize that appears in your outstretched hands. The ear contains a number of kernel equal to your Wisdom modifier (minimum of one). The kernels are different colors: blue, red, white, and yellow. You determine the ear's color composition when you first grow it. You may have any combination of colors, including an ear with kernels of the same color. The kernels last for one day or until you regain spells, whichever comes first, before they deteriorate and become useless.

As a standard action, you or another creature can detach a kernel from the cob and eat it. Alternatively, you or another creature can detach a kernel from the cob and give it to another creature as part of the same action, provided the giving creature has sufficient movement to reach the receiving creature. When a creature eats a kernel, the kernel's color determines its effects as follows:

Blue: A blue kernel allows the eater to hold his breath for 30 minutes.

Red: A red kernel has an extraordinarily sweet taste. For the next hour, the creature has a +2 on Charisma-based checks when interacting with animals, elementals, fey, and plants.

White: A white kernel ends either one disease or removes one curse affecting the creature with a DC less than or equal to 10 + your Druid level.

Yellow: A yellow kernel enhances the eater's endurance. For the next hour, the creature has a +2 on Constitution checks. In addition, when the creature fails a Fortitude saving throw, it can use an immediate action to redouble its stamina to resist the undesirable effect. Instead, of being subjected to the effect

resulting from the failed saving throw, the creature is instead blinded until the end of its next turn. When used in this way, the yellow kernel's effects immediately cease. Furthermore, the creature becomes immune to the yellow kernel's effects for eight hours after using it in the preceding manner.

Once you use this feature, you cannot use it again until you regain spells. This ability replaces wild empathy and woodland stride.

Crop Circle. (Su) At 6th level, you gain the ability to conjure maize. As an action, you choose a point you can see within 100 feet capable of supporting plant life. Within a 40-foot radius centered on that point, eight-foot-tall cornstalks instantly spring up from the ground, impeding travel and vision. A creature moving through the area must spend four feet of movement for every one foot it moves, and the area acts as cover, though creatures tall enough to peer over the cornstalks treat the area as partial cover instead. You can exclude one or more areas of any size within the crop circle from being affected. If you use crop circle on ground unsuitable for plant life — such as worked stone or open water — the effect fails and the attempted use is lost.

The cornstalks are ordinary plants that can be damaged and cleared away. They have Hardness 3 and 10 hit points per each five-foot square. Reducing a five-foot square to 0 hit points destroys the cornstalks, ending the crop circle's impediments to movement and vision in the area where the cornstalks have been destroyed. Cornstalks that have not been destroyed disintegrate into dust one hour after you conjure them.

You may use this ability once per day. This ability replaces the use of wild shape gained at 6th level.

Two with the Maize. (Su) At 10th level, the maize kernels created by your One with the Maize class feature gain the following properties in addition to those they already have:

Blue: The creature who eats a blue kernel gains the Amphibious trait and a swim speed equal to its base speed.

Red: Animals, elementals, fey, and plants are reluctant to attack a creature who eats the red kernel. When any of the preceding creatures target the eater with an attack or a harmful spell, they must succeed on a Will saving throw where the DC is 10 + half your Druid level + your Wisdom modifier. On a failed save, the attacker suffers a -5 penalty on its attack roll, while the creature who ate the red kernel has a +5 on its saving throw against a harmful spell cast by the attacker. A creature that successfully saves is immune to that red kernel's effects for 1 hour.

White: Ingesting a white kernel causes the eater to regain a number of hit points equal to double your druid level + your Wisdom modifier. In addition, the white kernel also ends one condition affecting the eater. The condition can be blinded, deafened, paralyzed, or poisoned.

Yellow: Eating a yellow kernel either removes one temporary negative level or ends any reduction to one of the eater's ability scores.

This ability replaces the use of wild shape gained at 10th level.

Maize Stride. **(Su)** At 14th level, you gain the ability to enter a maize plant in a manner akin to prying apart a corn husk and move from inside it to inside another maize plant within 250 feet. The maize plants must be living and at least tall enough to accommodate your height while standing upright. You must use five feet of movement to enter the maize plant. You instantly know the location of all other maize plants within 250 feet and, as part of the move used to enter the maize plant, can either pass into one of those maize plants or step out of the maize plant you are in. You appear in a spot of your choice within five feet of the destination maize plant, using another five feet of movement. If you have no movement left, you appear within five feet of the maize plant you entered.

You can use this transportation ability once per round for the next minute. You must end each turn outside a maize plant. Once you use this feature, you cannot use it again until you regain spells. This ability replaces the use of wild shape gained at 14th level.

FIGHTER ARCHETYPES

In almost every culture, armies have shaped the course of history. Leaders receive the overwhelming majority of credit for victories on the field of battle, yet their triumphs would be impossible if not for the fighting skill of the men and women serving under their command. Fighters form the backbone of nearly every military force ever assembled. Although renowned for their versatility, fighters ultimately specialize in a chosen martial discipline. Some use training and brute force to allow them to wield weapons with deadly precision and devastating effect. Others treat combat as an academic pursuit where they learn a variety of tactics and maneuvers to increase their odds of success on the battlefield. Some combatants even dabble in magic to enhance their martial prowess. Regardless of their chosen path, the brave warriors who win the day against their adversaries become heroes among the average person who can best relate to soldiers likely plucked from among their ranks than priests and magicians hailing from royalty or the aristocracy. While a legendary fighter may ascend to greatness from any economic class in Tehuatl, many learn their craft in the calmecac, a school catering to the sons of the elite.

ANIMAL CUAUHOCELOTL

Soldiers who distinguish themselves on the battlefield earn a coveted spot within their homeland's cuauhocelotl orders. These martial groups are associated with beasts indigenous to the island. In addition to earning the colorful, distinctive garb affiliated with a cuauhocelotl order, each of these prestigious organizations offers specialized training to its members that emulate the traits of its beastly namesake. Coyote cuauhocelotls value stealth and resourcefulness. Eagle cuauhocelotls enjoy enhanced perception. Jaguar cuauhocelotls hone their predatory instincts. Serpent cuauhocelotls prize guile and deception. In open battle, each of these orders proudly wears their colorful skins, though coyote cuauhocelotls and serpent cuauhocelotls often hide their allegiance to a cuauhocelotl order during a clandestine mission.

Bravado. Starting at 2nd level, Tehuatl cuauhocelotls proudly display their courage on the battlefield in an attempt to demoralize their opponents. When you do so, you can use an Attack of Opportunity to lower your guard to an opponent's melee weapon attack against you, granting that opponent a +2 on its attack roll. If the opponent's attack does not reduce you to 0 hit points, impose a condition that prevents you from taking an action, or cause you to become demoralized, the target becomes demoralized. At the end of each of its subsequent turns, the target can make a Will saving throw with a DC of 10 + your Intimidate bonus. On a success, the target is no longer demoralized. If the opponent's initial melee attack missed you, the demoralized foe increases the DC to end the effect to 20 + your Intimidate bonus. You can use this ability a number of times per day equal to an ability score modifier that you use for the Intimidate skill. This replaces Bravery.

Cuauhocelotl Order. At 2nd level, you undergo the rituals and tests required to join a cuauhocelotl order. Choose one of the following cuauhocelotl orders:

Coyote: Cleverness and opportunism rank among the coyote cuauhocelotl's prized traits, while discretion may be the better part of valor under less-than-ideal circumstances. Despite the preceding philosophy, abandoning a friend during combat disgraces the order. Spying also comes naturally to the wily coyote. Stealth becomes a class skill for you, and you have a bonus on Stealth checks made while wearing light or no armor equal to half your class level.

Eagle: Keen observation rather than rash reactions win the day. Eagle cuauhocelotls take in their surroundings and then carefully assess every situation. Withdrawal is an acceptable alternative when faced with a superior adversary. An impulsive action that imperils others violates the eagle cuauhocelotl's core values. Eagle cuauhocelotls see what others miss. Perception becomes a class skill for you, and you have a bonus on Perception checks that rely on sight equal to 1/4 your class level.

Jaguar: Preparation is more important than participation. The always calculating jaguar determines when and where to fight. When the time and place are ideal, there can be no surrender nor retreat. With experience, the jaguar cuauhocelotl's predatory senses and agility greatly improve. Acrobatics becomes a class skill for you, and you have a bonus on Acrobatics and Climb checks equal to half your class level.

Serpent. None can defeat you except yourself. Pain offers the path to vanquishing fear. The serpent's scales must be pierced to reveal the cuauhocelotl's true mettle. When the serpent conquers fear, anything becomes possible. Absent the trepidation of failure, trickery and treachery hold the keys to victory. These cuauhocelotls undergo a gruesome scarification ritual that transforms you into a fearless soldier. You regain the Bravery class feature.

Once you select a cuauhocelotlly order, you cannot change it. If you commit a transgression that violates the tenets of your order, such as displaying cowardice on the battlefield, you do not gain any additional cuauhocelotlly order features until you make amends for your sin by redeeming yourself in battle or through magical redemption such as an *atonement* or similar magic. This replaces your bonus feat at 2nd level.

Improved Cuauhocelotl Order. At 6th level, your cuauhocelotl order bestows the following additional benefits.

Coyote: You learn to attack in the manner of your beastly namesake. You gain 1d6 Sneak Attack damage. This is exactly like the rogue ability of the same name. The extra damage dealt increases by +1d6 every six levels (6th, 12th, and 18th). If a Coyote Cuauhocelotl gets a sneak attack bonus from another source, the bonuses on damage stack.

Eagle: Your visual senses detect the minutest details. You gain the Blind-Fight feat. In addition, you gain Improved Blind-Fight at 12th level and Greater Blind-Fight at 18th level.

Jaguar: You develop the hunting skills of a predatory cat. If you charge at least 20 feet straight toward a creature and then hit it with a melee attack, you may make an additional attack against it with a -5 penalty. At 12th level, you may make a second additional attack with a -10 penalty. At 18th level, you may make a third additional attack at a -15 penalty.

Serpent: You speak with forked tongue and can twist words beyond recognition. Bluff and Disguise becomes class skills for you, and you have a bonus on Bluff and Disguise checks equal to half your class level. Additionally, your Bravery class feature now applies to all Will saving throws.

This replaces your bonus feats at 6th, 12th, and 18th level.

Higher Orders. At 20th level, you become one with your order, reaching the zenith of your orderly powers. Each order gains the following abilities:

Coyote: You can skulk into the background, allowing you to quickly disappear from sight. You gain the rogue talent Hide in Plain Sight for all terrains.

Eagle: Your visual acuity reaches unprecedented heights. You gain constant *see invisibility* as an extraordinary ability.

Jaguar: You master the ability to run down your prey. Your move speed doubles whenever you take the charge or run actions.

Serpent: You master fear and can conquer all. Your Bravery class feature now applies to all attack rolls, ability checks, initiative checks, and saving throws.

This replaces your bonus feat at 20th level.

OMATI

Renowned for their fearlessness, these warriors represent the elite core of soldiers. Devotees of Yaocteotl, the god of war, the Omati display their combat prowess through their elaborate dress and stylish weaponry. They usually occupy the front ranks of any military force in Tehuatl. While most soldiers fight to kill their opponents, their deity demands the blood of the living rather than fallen corpses. In pursuit of this desired goal, the Omati actively attempt to capture their adversaries instead of slay them outright and move onto the next waiting opponent. The Omati use a variety of techniques to accomplish the tasks, ranging from the patently simple method of knocking an enemy unconscious with a blow to the head to the extremely intricate maneuver of targeting a nerve cluster. What some may mistake as an act of mercy is in reality a far worse fate than death on the battlefield.

Resistance is Futile. **(Ex)** At 1st level, you discover the effects of charm and deception on the battlefield. You add Bluff, Diplomacy, and Disguise to you class skills and gain 2 additional skill ranks each level. This ability replaces the bonus feat gained at 1st level and alters class skills.

Take Prisoners. At 2nd level, you learn specialized techniques designed to hasten an opponent's capture or incapacitation. When you gain this feature, you learn one Take Prisoner option of your choice (see "Take Prisoner Options" below). A Take Prisoner option can be applied to a melee weapon attack dealing the same damage type (bludgeoning, piercing, or slashing) as the selected option. For instance, you cannot apply a Take Prisoner option for bludgeoning damage to a melee attack dealing slashing damage.

Once per turn, when you make a melee weapon attack against a humanoid or animal, you can apply one of your Take Prisoner options to the attack. You decide to use the option when the attack hits the humanoid or animal. You have a number of uses of this ability equal to your Fighter level per day.

You gain an additional Take Prisoners option of your choice when you reach certain levels in this class: 6th, 10th, and 14th level.

This ability replaces the bonus feats gained at 2nd, 6th, 10th, and 14th level.

Seize the Advantage. At 7th level, you can quickly pounce on a reeling opponent to knock your foe unconscious rather than kill it. When a humanoid or animal fails its saving throw against your Take Prisoners feature, you can use a swift action to make a melee weapon attack against that creature. If the attack reduces the creature to 0 or less hit points, you can knock out the creature, rendering it unconscious and stable at -1 hit points. If you elect to kill the humanoid or beast instead, your actions displease the hero-gods. As punishment, you lose your Take Prisoners class feature until the following dawn. This ability replaces the armor training increase at 7th level.

Willing Prisoner. At 9th level, you discover words can be more effective than weapons. You can use your standard action to *charm* a humanoid or animal that you can see within 30 feet of you. If the creature can see and hear you, it must succeed on a Will saving throw where the DC is equal to 10 + half your Fighter level + your Charisma modifier or be *charmed* as *charm person* until the end of your next turn. You can use your move action on subsequent turns to extend the duration of this effect on the charmed creature until the end of your next turn. This effect ends if the target ends its turn out of your sight or more than 30 feet from you. Likewise, if you or your companions do anything harmful to it, the effect ends. If the creature you choose does not understand the same language as you, it is unaffected by this feature. A creature who succeeds on its saving throw and one that has been harmed by you or your companions cannot be affected by your use of this feature for 24 hours.

You can use this feature a number of times per day equal to your Charisma modifier (minimum once). This ability replaces the weapon training increase at 9th level.

Sense Blood. At 15th level, you can follow up on a devastating blow. When you score a critical hit on a melee weapon attack against an animal or humanoid, you can apply a Take Prisoners option to the attack without expending a use of the feature. This ability replaces the armor training increase at 15th level.

TAKE PRISONERS OPTIONS

The Take Prisoners feature allows you to select options for it at certain levels. Each option applies to a specific damage type. If an option requires a saving throw, your Take Prisoners save DC equals 10 + half your Fighter level + your Charisma modifier.

Body Blow (bludgeoning damage): Your weapon strikes your opponent's vulnerable spot, sapping its energy. The target must succeed on a Fortitude saving throw or gain the fatigued condition. When you reach 18th level in this class, the target gains the exhausted condition instead.

Eye Gouge (piercing damage). You poke your opponent in the eye with the pointed end of your weapon. The target must succeed on a Fortitude saving throw or become blinded. At the end of each of its turns, the target can make another Fortitude saving throw. On a success, the target is no longer blinded. When you reach 18th level in this class, the target also takes 2d6 damage.

Hamstring (slashing damage): Your blade slices through a vital ligament, muscle, or tendon to inhibit your target's movement. The target must succeed on a Fortitude saving throw or its mobility is impaired. The target's speed is halved, it suffers a -2 penalty on Reflex saving throws, and it cannot use immediate actions. At the end of each of its turns, the target can make another Fortitude saving throw. On a success, the effect ends, allowing the target to move and act normally. When you reach 18th level in this class, the target's speed is reduced to five feet, and it is staggered.

Knockout Blow (bludgeoning damage): You use the flat part of your weapon to deal a concussive blow to your adversary. The target must succeed on a Fortitude saving throw or be stunned until the end of your next turn. When you reach 18th level in this class, the target also takes 2d6 damage.

Nerve Cluster (piercing damage): The tip of your weapon rips through a crucial nerve bundle. The target must succeed on a Fortitude saving throw or be entangled and anchored. At the end of each of the target's turns, the target can make another Fortitude saving throw. On a success, the target is no longer entangled. When you reach 18th level in this class, the target also takes 2d6 damage.

Tripping Strike (bludgeoning, piercing, or slashing): You knock the feet out from under your opponent. The target must succeed on a Reflex saving throw or be knocked prone. When you reach 18th level in this class, you can use your attack of opportunity to perform this feature against the target if it is within reach and attempting to stand up from prone.

Wing Clip (slashing damage): You sever the muscles allowing a winged opponent to take flight. The target must succeed on a Fortitude saving throw or lose its flying speed. At the end of each of the target's turns, the target can make another Fortitude saving throw. On a success, the target regains its flying speed. This option only affects flying creatures that rely solely on their wings to take flight. When you reach 18th level in this class, the target also takes 2d6 damage.

MONK ARCHETYPES

Monks are living weapons and fountains of enlightenment who draw their power from a mystical source presumably tied to their lifeforce. They use discipline, exercise, and contemplation to transform their bodies into instruments of devastation and introspection. While most adventurers see their lives as a series of unrelated, random episodes, monks view their existence as a journey along a designated path toward spiritual fulfillment. Every action they take builds toward a greater purpose within the universe's grand scheme. Although monks hone their minds and bodies in preparation for war, many use their power and skills to advocate for peace. In pursuit of this endeavor, monks generally eschew the trappings of wealth and power. Instead, they lead a simple, ascetic lifestyle devoid of worldly distractions and pretenses. Humility and insight are the tools in their arsenal as they endeavor to persuade others to walk down the road to inner tranquility alongside them. Some detractors erroneously mistake the monk's reluctance to resort to violence for strict pacifism. However, when the need arises, these fierce warriors let their fists, feet, and weapons speak for them. In pursuit of these martial endeavors, monks adhere to the tenets of a monastic tradition typically associated with a fighting style or a philosophy.

MACUAHUITL

In Tehuatl, no weapon strikes more terror in the heart of an enemy than the vicious macuahuitl. From its fearsome appearance to its razor-sharp edges, this stony version of the longsword may be more brittle than traditional steel, but its ability to easily rip through flesh and tissue remains unmatched. The monks who devote their singular focus to the intricacies of this vicious blade become one with their macuahuitl. They perceive the weapon as the tangible manifestation of their own consciousness. It moves in sync with its living partner, seemingly transitioning from offense to defense in the blink of an eye. In the hands of these monks, the inanimate object takes on a life of its own.

Macuahuitl Master. **(Ex)** The macuahuitl is a monk weapon for you. Although the weapon normally deals slashing damage, you can choose to have it deal bludgeoning damage instead, though when you do so, you suffer a -2 penalty on your attack rolls. This ability alters weapon proficiency.

Surgical Strike. **(Ex)** At 4th level, your macuahuitl becomes a deadly instrument of death. When you hit another creature with your macuahuitl, you can spend 1 ki point to rip open a grievous wound. If the target is a creature other than a construct or an undead, it must succeed on a Fortitude saving throw where the DC equals 10 + half your Monk level + your Wisdom modifier or take bleed damage equal to your Monk level. You can use this feature only once on each of your turns. You can use this feature only when your macuahuitl deals slashing damage.

This ability replaces the ki power gained at 4th level (unchained monk) or slow fall (CRB monk).

Defensive Posture. **(Ex)** Starting at 6th level, you can use your macuahuitl to defend yourself. When you are hit by a melee attack, you can spend 1 ki point as an immediate action to use your macuahuitl to block the incoming strike. When you do so, your macuahuitl must be in your hand and you cannot be incapacitated. The damage you take is reduced by 1d8 + your Strength modifier + your monk level. If you reduced the damage to 0, you may spend 1 ki point to make a melee attack against the creature that hit you as part of the same action. This ability replaces the bonus feat gained at 6th level.

Obsidian Shards. **(Su)** At 12th level, you gain the ability to unleash a cone of serrated obsidian wedges. As a standard action, your macuahuitl, which must be in your hand, instantly conjures a 20-foot cone of tiny, wedge-shaped obsidian chips with lethal edges. Each creature in the cone must succeed on a Reflex saving throw where the DC equals 10 + half your Monk level + your Wisdom modifier or take 3d6 slashing damage or half as much damage on a successful saving throw. You can increase the cone's damage by spending ki points. Each point you spend, to a maximum of 2, increases the damage by 3d6. This ability replaces the ki power gained at 12th level (unchained monk) or abundant step (CRB monk).

Pain of Death. **(Su)** At 17th level, your macuahuitl earns its reputation as a killing machine. When you hit a target with your macuahuitl, the weapon deals extra negative energy damage to the target equal to your Monk level. You can use this feature only once on each of your turns. This ability replaces timeless body.

NETOTILO

Dancing plays an important ceremonial role during warfare, yet some practitioners have taken the discipline to the next step. They choreograph the rhythmic movements into a lethal martial art imbued with mystical energy. Each twist, turn, leap, and pivot mimics an ordinary dance routine, but the combination of swirling motions and gestures pack a devastating punch for any opponent attempting to cut in on the action. To enhance their combat prowess, these monks also develop a knack for fighting from unorthodox positions. Although they can dance without audible sound, they reach their full potential when they can draw power from music. Nothing can stop one of these monks when they hear a captivating beat pulsating in the background.

Netotilo Steps. **(Ex)** At 3rd level, you learn three steps you can add into your Flurry of Blows, total defense, or charge. These steps have the following effects:

Ecatl: Whenever you charge, you can use your immediate action to move up to half your speed whenever a creature you can see or hear within 30 feet of you casts a spell with a somatic or verbal component. If you do not use your action before the start of your next turn, it is lost.

Otlipantili: Whenever you use Flurry of Blows, you can use your immediate action to make an unarmed strike against a creature within reach that attacks or harms you before the start of your next turn.

Tapalcayotl: Whenever you use total defense, you can use your immediate action to give you a +2 on one Fortitude or Reflex saving throw before the start of your next turn.

This ability replaces the fast movement increase gained at third level.

Turn the Beat Around. **(Ex)** Starting at 6th level, your dancing teaches you to move and fight from awkward positions other than an upright stance. You can use one of the following techniques on each of your turns:

Campaztca: While squeezing through a smaller space you do not suffer the penalties for squeezing.

Techoponia: While prone, you can crawl at half your move speed without penalty and do not suffer the penalties for being prone.

Tlanna: While entangles, you do not suffer the penalties for being entangled.

You can use one of the preceding benefits on each of your turns. Therefore, if you are squeezing through a smaller space while prone, you can use campaztca technique or the techoponia technique, but not both. This ability replaces the bonus feat gained at 6th level.

Dancing Queen. **(Su)** At 12th level, your mind can process any sound as a rhythmic beat. As a swift action, you can spend 2 ki points to immediately gain the benefits of *freedom of movement* for one turn, provided you can hear audible noise louder than a whisper. You cannot use this feature if you or the area you occupy is silenced. This ability replaces the ki power gained at 12th level (unchained monk) or abundant step (CRB monk).

I Believe I Can Fly. **(Su)** At 18th level, you can temporarily slip the bonds of earth and soar into the skies. As a swift action, you can spend 1 ki point to allow you to fly until the end of your next turn. You gain a fly speed equal to your base move speed (perfect). This replaces the bonus feat gained at 18th level.

PALADIN OATHS

The people of Tehuatl refer to those who fight for righteousness and order as exalted heroes rather than using the term "paladin", though the term still applies to the character class within the context of the game's rules system. They serve as the vanguards spearheading the eternal struggle against wickedness and disorder. Exalted heroes upholding their noble ideals never compromise their lofty principles. For them, the straight and narrow path never diverges. These holy warriors of lawfulness and goodness expect others to trace their exact footsteps because their road is the only one leading to salvation. They perceive themselves as a hopeful, guiding light amid the darkness of sin. Through force of arms and devout faith, they swear to vanquish chaos and evil from the world around them. Regardless of the odds against them, exalted heroes never surrender nor retreat even when their enemies threaten to engulf them. Many lands and worlds owe their survival to the heroic sacrifices made by these staunch bastions of justice. To aid them in their cause, exalted heroes profess their beliefs and ideals through their commitment to a solemn oath. Their sacred vow shapes the tools and weapons at their disposal in their quest to triumph over their foes. Aztli exalted heroes generally value time-honored traditions and beliefs more than codified laws or religious doctrines. Some of Tehuatl's other races place more emphasis on fighting against a hated enemy or defending their people against an external threat.

OATH OF IDEALISM

Humility in the home — pride on the battlefield. That is the motto of huehuetlatolli. These paladins abide by the sayings of the old people who have passed down their people's traditions for countless generations.

TENETS OF IDEALISM

Family First: None can sever the bonds of family. Respect your elders, value your siblings, cherish your partner, and love your children.

Piety: Honor and appease the gods. All bounties come from their generosity.

Due Diligence: Work hard and obey those above your station.

Fall with Grace: Never show fear, never surrender, and always fight until your last breath. Accepting cowardice is a fate worse than death.

TABLE C-1: OATH OF IDEALISM SPELLS

Spell Level	Spells
1st	*command*
2nd	*heroism*
3rd	*blessing of fervor*
4th	*banishment*

Appease the Gods. **(Su)** Starting at 4th level, as a standard action, you present your holy symbol and demand an offering to the gods, using two uses of your Lay On Hands. Each creature of your choice, other than constructs, that you can see within 30 feet of you must succeed on a Will saving throw against your Lay On Hands DC. On a failed save, the creature uses its immediate action, if it hasn't used it already, to fall prone. On its next turn, the target, if it has not fallen prone before the start of its turn, must use its swift action to fall prone. The target then must use its standard action to drop whatever it is holding as tributes to the gods. The creature remains prone and cannot retrieve the dropped objects until it takes damage or until a creature other than you takes possession of its offerings. The creature can repeat the Will saving throw at the end of each of its turns, ending the effect on itself with a success. This ability replaces channel energy.

Free Will. **(Su)** Starting at 5th level, you can use two uses of your Lay On Hands to bolster courage and reassert individualism. As a swift action, each creature of your choice that you can see within 40 feet of you may use their immediate action to immediately make a new saving throw, if applicable, against a spell or magical effect that charmed or frightened them. The new saving throw also applies to ongoing spells and magical effects that do not affect creatures that cannot be charmed or frightened. This ability replaces divine bond.

Aura of Industry. **(Su)** Starting at 8th level, your industrious work ethic inspires others to match your effort and intensity. You are immune to fatigue and allies within 10 feet of you cannot suffer from fatigue or exhaustion while you are conscious. This ability replaces aura of resolve.

Exude Courage. **(Su)** At 17th level, you gain temporary hit points equal to your Charisma modifier (minimum 1) at the start of each of your turns. You lose any remaining temporary hit points from the previous round at the start of each of your turns. This ability replaces aura of righteousness.

Humility. **(Su)** At 20th level, you exemplify Tehuatl's grandest ideals, giving you protection from most attacks. Any creature who targets you with an attack or a harmful spell must succeed on a Will saving throw where the DC is equal to 10 + half your Paladin level + your Charisma modifier. On a failed Will saving throw, the creature must choose a new target or lose the attack or spell. This feature does not protect you against area effects. If you attack a creature, cast a spell on it, deal damage to it, that creature is immune to this feature until you next regain spells. This ability replaces holy champion.

OATH OF SACRIFICE

Outsiders misconstrue this oath as the paladin's pledge to sacrifice other creatures' lives or property. Instead, the holy warriors who accept this vow believe in the virtues of intentional self-deprivation and martyrdom.

TENETS OF SACRIFICE

Bear Another's Burden: Understanding cannot come without suffering.
Charity: The act of giving is more rewarding than receiving.
Fidelity: The needs of others outweigh self-interest.
One Life for Many: Selfishness leads to dishonor. Those who lose everything gain the most.

TABLE C–2: OATH OF SACRIFICE SPELLS

Spell Level	Spells
1st	*false life*
2nd	*final sacrifice*
3rd	*guardian of faith*
4th	*hallow*

Retributive Martyrdom. (Su) Starting at 3rd level, you can use your Lay On Hands to transfer the suffering of others onto yourself. If the target is blinded, charmed, deafened, frightened, paralyzed, petrified, poisoned, or stunned, this ability ends the condition affecting the target. If the target suffers from more than one condition, you choose the condition to end. The condition previously affecting the target now affects you instead. In addition, if the creature that caused the condition on the original target is within 30 feet of you, it must succeed on a Will saving throw against your Lay on Hands DC. On a failed Will saving throw, your act of selflessness deals 2d6 positive energy damage to that creature, and half as much damage on a successful Will saving throw. This ability replaces the mercy gained at 3rd level.

Indomitable. (Su) Starting at 6th level, whenever you use your Retributive Martyrdom you gain a divine bonus to all Constitution checks and Fortitude saves equal to the number of dice your Lay on Hands rolled until the end of your next turn. This ability replaces the mercy gained at 6th level.

Step in Your Shoes. (Su) Beginning at 7th level, you can thrust yourself into danger to aid others. When a friendly creature within five feet of you takes damage or is visibly harmed by a spell or magical effect, you can use an attack of opportunity to swap positions with the target. If the creature took damage from the attack, effect, or spell, you magically half the damage, and the creature takes half the damage. This feature does not transfer any other effect that might accompany the damage, and this damage cannot be reduced in any way. This ability replaces the use of smite evil gained at 7th level.

Ultimate Sacrifice. (Su) Starting at 15th level, when you are reduced to 0 hit points or less and are not killed outright, you can choose to make the ultimate sacrifice. When you do so, each friendly creature within 20 feet of you regains hit points equal to double your paladin level. When you use this feature, you leave your fate in the hands of the gods. You cannot be stabilized or healed by any means, including through spells, ability checks, and magical effects. Instead, you must make a Fortitude save to determine your fate, where the DC is equal to 10 + half your Paladin level + your Charisma modifier. If you die, friendly creatures within 20 feet of you regain an additional 2d6 hit points. Once you use this feature, you cannot use it again until you regain spells. This ability replaces the mercy gained at 15th level.

Selflessness. (Su) At 18th level, you place the needs of others above your own. You may now use your Lay on Hands at will, though your touch can heal only other creatures, not yourself. This ability replaces the mercy gained at 18th level.

RANGER ARCHETYPES

Generals and troops perceive nature as an obstacle at best and an adversary at worst. Conversely, rangers see nature as a trusted friend and ally. These wilderness warriors use the terrain and its inhabitants to their maximum advantage, emulating some traits consistent with the land's most successful bestial killers. While the soil and vegetation can stop a conventional army dead in its tracks, the ranger often moves across the same ground without impediment. Like their animal counterparts, rangers consider themselves to be hunters instead of soldiers. They devote their energies toward the study and mastery over a designated category of foes, a unique environment, and a fighting style, much like a predator targeting its favored prey. Because of their specialized set of skills, some military units tab rangers to serve as scouts or skirmishers. However, most rangers prefer operating alone rather than working at the behest of someone else. They function best as individuals or parts of small cohesive groups, where their mobility gives them a decided leg up on their enemies. In addition to their unhampered movement, rangers also complement their specialized combat skills with a limited repertoire of spells designed to enhance their strength suits in the wilderness.

AXOLOTL

Named after the salamander bearing the same name, these warriors usually operate alongside the canal separating the Aztli Confederation from their southern neighbors, though they can also be found in swampy terrain across the island. Naturally their affinity for water enhances their aquatic expertise, which prompts some landlubbers to derogatorily refer to them as "fishmen" or "merfolk." Despite the monikers, axolotls move with astounding grace on dry land as they swiftly and silently dispatch enemies standing in their way. Because of their concentration near the canal, Aztlis and Poqozas make up the vast majority of these rangers operating in Tehuatl. Axolotls generally operate as part of a specialized unit within an established military force, yet some use their specialized abilities to enrich themselves as adventurers or to cause trouble around one of the many hotspots along the canal.

Reconnaissance. (Ex) At 2nd level you gain one of the following features of your choice:

Debilitate: You have a +4 on CMB checks to pin a creature you are grappling. If you successfully pin the creature, the target must also succeed on a Fortitude saving throw where the DC is equal to 10 + your Ranger level + Wisdom modifier. On a failed Fortitude saving throw, a creature is knocked unconscious. At the end of each of its turns, the creature can make another Fortitude saving throw. On a success, the creature is no longer unconscious, though it remains grappled if you or another creature did not end the grapple.

Go It Alone: You are at your best when fighting alone. When you hit a creature with a melee attack and no friendly creatures are threatening the creature you hit, the creature takes an extra 1d6 precision damage from the successful attack. The extra damage increases to 2d6 at 9th level, and 3d6 at 17th level.

Reconnoiter: You excel at avoiding detection and spotting hidden danger. You double the bonus on Stealth checks and Perception checks made in your favored terrain.

This ability replaces the combat style feat gained at 2nd level.

Locomotion. (Ex) At 6th level, you gain an alternate mode of location. You choose either a climb speed or a swim speed equal to your base speed. This ability replaces the combat style feat gained at 6th level.

Commando. (Ex) At 10th level, you gain one of the following features of your choice:

Desperate Measures: You can use a standard action to make a wild swing with a bludgeoning or slashing weapon that you hold in your hand. Each creature within five feet of you must succeed on a Reflex saving throw where the DC is equal to 10 + your Ranger level + Wisdom modifier. On a failed Reflex saving throw, the creature takes bludgeoning or slashing damage equal to the weapon's normal damage + your ranger level, and its speed is reduced to 0. On a successful Reflex saving throw, the creature takes half as much damage and its speed is not reduced. At the end of each of its turns, the creature can make another Reflex saving throw. On a success, the creature's speed returns to normal. You can use this feature once per hour.

Tuck and Roll: Whenever an opponent misses a ranged attack against you or if you succeed on a Reflex saving throw, you may use your immediate action to move up to 10 feet, fall prone, or both. If your movement provokes an opportunity attack, the opponent suffers a -4 penalty on the attack.

This ability replaces the combat style feat gained at 10th level.

Master Strategist. (Ex) At 14th level, you gain one of the following features of your choice:

Formulate Plan: Your powers of observation serve you well. You can spend one round carefully surveying the actions of creatures you can see. Once you have spent one minute doing so, you gain the following benefits against the creatures you observed for the next one minute:

Subjects cannot make opportunity attacks against you.

When you take damage from a subject's attack, you can use your immediate action to either make one melee weapon attack against the creature that hit you or reduce the damage dealt by an amount equal to your levels in this class. You must use this feature before you know the outcome of the damage roll.

Seal: You become an expert aquatic combatant. You gain the Amphibious trait. If you have a swim speed and swim at least 10 feet straight toward a target, any creature you hit with a melee attack on the same turn must succeed on a Fortitude saving throw where the DC is equal to 10 + your Ranger level + Wisdom modifier or inadvertently swallow water. A creature that swallows water is staggered while it coughs and chokes. At the end of each of its turns, the target can make another Fortitude saving throw. On a success, it is no longer staggered.

This ability replaces the combat style feat gained at 14th level.

Combat Feat. (Ex) At 18th level, you gain one combat feat of your choice. This ability replaces the combat style feat gained at 18th level.

TITLANTLI

Information is power, and these tireless couriers are the conduits for its dissemination across Tehuatl. While most societies rely upon mounted riders to deliver messages and communiques throughout the land, the island lacks these resources and must instead depend upon humanoid runners to perform the same arduous tasks. Stamina and speed are naturally key attributes for these individuals, but theirs is a dangerous life. People and creatures sometimes stand in their way, including those intentionally trying to disrupt communications and others lying in wait looking for what they perceive to be an easy target. For the titlantli, reaching their destination safely takes precedence over getting there as quickly as possible. To avoid ambushes, booby traps, and thieves, titlantlis must frequently take the road never traveled, forcing them to venture along circuitous routes through untamed wilderness, potentially taking them into hazardous, uncharted areas.

Run Like the Wind. (Ex) At 1st level, your speed increases by 10 feet while you are not wearing heavy armor. This bonus increases to 15 feet when you reach 8th level and 20 feet when you reach 15th level. This ability replaces the favored enemy progression at 1st level.

Titlantli Magic. (Sp) Starting at 4th level, you learn an additional spell when you reach certain levels in this class as shown in the Titlantli Spells table. The spell counts as a ranger spell for you, but it can be spontaneously cast. You can "lose" any prepared spell in order to cast any of the following spells of the same spell level or lower. This ability alters spellcasting and replaces the favored enemy progression at 5th and 20th level.

TABLE C-3: TITLANTLI SPELLS

Ranger Level	Spell	Spell Level
4th	expeditious retreat	1st
7th	alter self	2nd
10th	haste	3rd
13th	polymorph	4th

Road Not Traveled. (Ex) At 8th level, your extensive travels take you outside your comfort zone, bringing you into unfamiliar territory. While traveling for an hour or more in terrain that is not your favored terrain, you can treat the terrain as favored terrain (+2) until you rest. Once you choose a terrain, you cannot change it for the rest of the day. You can use this ability once per day. This ability replaces the favored terrain gained at 8th level.

Marathoner. (Ex) At 8th level, your stamina reaches new heights. You can move at your normal speed for up to 12 hours a day without suffering exhaustion from a forced march. Furthermore, you gain a +5 on checks to avoid fatigue and exhaustion. This ability replaces swift tracker.

Parting Shot. (Ex) At 10th level, you master the art of hit-and-run fighting. Immediately after you hit an opponent with an attack, you can take a swift action to take the Disengage action, for up to a maximum of double your speed moved in total for the round. This ability replaces the favored enemy progression at 10th level.

Determined. (Ex) At 15th level, you are singularly focused on the task at hand. If another creature forces you to make a Will saving throw, provided you are not already immune to the effect, you can use your immediate action to

make one weapon attack against that creature. If your attack hits, your saving throw automatically succeeds in addition to dealing the attack's normal effects. If you score a critical hit on the attack, the target is stunned until the end of its next turn. This ability replaces the favored enemy progression at 15th level.

ROGUE ARCHETYPES

Anyone who decides to become a rogue embraces an eclectic way of life unfettered by the constraints of annoying rules and expectations. Indeed, rogues are best defined by the diverse repertoire of skills they use to ply their trades. They are chameleons equally capable of talking someone into voluntarily giving them their life's savings or stealing those same valuables from right under their nose, leaving their mark none the wiser. They rely upon wit, agility, and guile to survive in a perilous environment teeming with shady characters living along the edges of legality. Despite their reputation for skullduggery, rogues are an invaluable asset to any adventuring party. No character class is better suited to wrest a heavily guarded treasure from its owner than a resourceful rogue who can dip into his seemingly endless bag of tricks. They excel at opening locked doors, fabricating disguises, walking along ledges, and disarming traps — just to name a few of their many talents. Rogues typically operate in the underbelly of humanoid settlements where they remain safely ensconced within the shadows, though some also conduct their business in the public eye while keeping their true identity a coveted secret.

POCHTECA

Commerce thrives in the numerous cities, villages, and towns scattered across Tehuatl. Yet the island's bustling trade industry could not exist without the efforts of its legions of pochtecas. These merchants discreetly move from settlement to settlement where they peddle their wares, including the latest gossip. Their extensive travels put them in contact with numerous individuals from various walks of life, both legal and illicit. Their access to confidential information and private quarters off limits to most make them valuable assets for political, religious, and economic interests seeking such details. For these reasons, the rich and powerful frequently employ them as spies. In this capacity, they observe their surroundings and report their findings to their superiors. Others are content being freelancers who use their knowledge and experience to the advantage of themselves instead of others.

Work the Crowd. (Ex) At 2nd level, you master the subtleties of finding reliable sources of goods and information. You have a +2 on Diplomacy checks made to locate the person with the best news, information, and gossip. If you spend 10 minutes interacting with or eavesdropping on people's discussions, you get a sense of the current buzz within the community. You learn basic details about the settlement's local customs and traditions, such as its form of government, economic system, and prominent religions as well as the populace's general attitude toward these institutions. This ability replaces the rogue talent gained at 2nd level.

Find Anything. (Sp) At 10th level, your acuity for finding people and objects imbues you with magical ability. When you do so, you can cast *locate creature* or *locate object* as spell-like abilities with a caster level equal to your character level. Charisma is your spellcasting ability for these spells. You can use this ability once per day for every 2 Rogue levels you possess. This ability replaces the rogue talent gained at 10th level.

Anonymity. (Su) Beginning at 14th level, your propensity for blending into a crowd reaches new heights. When you are targeted by an attack from a creature you can see, you can use your immediate action to magically force the attacker to succeed on a Will saving throw where the DC is equal to 10 + half your Rogue level + your Charisma modifier or lose you in the crowd. If you get lost in the crowd, the attacker must choose a new target or lose the attack or spell. You cannot use this feature against an attacker with an Intelligence score of 4 or less. A target that successfully saves on its Will saving throw is immune to your Anonymity feature for 24 hours. You can use this feature a number of times per day equal to your Charisma modifier (minimum of one). This ability replaces the rogue talent gained at 14th level.

Dealmaker. (Ex) At 18th level, your powers of persuasion reach their zenith. As a standard action, you can target a creature you can see. That creature must be able to hear you and the two of you must share a language. If you meet these conditions and succeed on a Diplomacy check contested by the target's Sense Motive check, the target becomes preoccupied listening to you for the next minute, provided you use your swift action on each of your subsequent turns to continue speaking. If you and your companions are fighting the creature, it has a +10 on its Sense Motive check. If you lose the contested check, the target is immune to your Dealmaker feature for the next hour.

While listening to you, the target is distracted for Perception checks made to perceive any creature other than you until the effect ends or the target can no longer hear you. Furthermore, your speech distracts the target. At the beginning of each of its turns, it must succeed on a concentration check to maintain concentration for a spell already in effect. If the target attempts to cast a spell requiring concentration, it must also succeed on its concentration check; otherwise, the spell fails and is lost. This feature has no effect on creatures with an Intelligence score of 4 or lower.

You can use this feature a number of times per day equal to your Charisma modifier (minimum of one). This ability replaces the rogue talent gained at 18th level.

Ullamaloni

The ball game plays an important role in Tehuatl society. Like the gladiators of ancient Rome, ullamalonis who excel on the ullamaliztli court can reach an exalted status. Yet, the speed, agility, and guile they bring to their sport translates well to adventuring. In some ways, exploring forsaken places or fighting hideous monsters may be less dangerous endeavors than participating in their chosen profession. Ullamalonis fare best when putting their physical talents to the test instead of trying their hands at the subtler aspects of being a rogue. Running up a wall or hurling a weapon at a small target play right into their wheelhouse. On the other hand, creating a disguise to slip past a night watchman proves problematic.

Hip Check. **(Ex)** Starting at 3rd level, your prowess at bouncing the ball off your hips allows you to make an unarmed strike with them. When you move at least 10 feet during your turn, you can use your swift action to make an unarmed strike with your hips. The creature you attacked cannot make opportunity attacks against you for the rest of your turn. This ability replaces trap sense.

Run the Walls. **(Ex)** At 4th level, you can literally walk parallel to the ground along an inclined surface, including on a sheer, vertical wall. Because you are walking and not climbing, your speed remains the same. You must walk along the surface at a height no greater than your own. Therefore, you cannot use this feature to climb or run up a surface. When you move at least 10 feet immediately before you mount the wall, you can move a number of feet equal to your Strength score. If you did not move at least 10 feet before walking on the wall, you can move a number of feet equal to your Strength modifier. Although you are walking on the wall, you still occupy the space adjacent to the wall. Your movement on the wall does not provoke opportunity attacks, and you end your movement on your feet. You cannot run the walls more than once per turn. This ability replaces uncanny dodge.

Thread the Needle. **(Ex)** At 8th level, you can move through and past opponents on the field of play and battle. You may use Climb in place of Acrobatics to move through an enemy's square. When you use Acrobatics or Climb to move through an enemy's square, you can use your swift action to make a melee attack against the target. This ability replaces improved uncanny dodge.

Dodge Ball. **(Ex)** Beginning at 12th level, you develop an uncanny knack for avoiding danger at the last second. When you are targeted by an attack, you can use your immediate action to move up to half your speed. The attack's outcome is not resolved until you end your movement, which may move you outside of the attack's range or provide you total cover. If the attacker can no longer target you after you move, the attack automatically fails. This movement does not provoke opportunity attacks. You can use this feature a number of times per day equal to your Wisdom modifier (minimum of one). This ability replaces the rogue talent gained at 12th level.

Heart of a Champion. **(Ex)** At 18th level, your unwillingness to accept defeat defines your character. If you fail a saving throw, you can roll it again with a +2. You can use this ability 3 times per day. This ability replaces the rogue talent gained at 18th level.

Sorcerer Archetypes

Magic originates from many sources. The blood of a legendary hero, a fearsome monster, or even a divine being may course through a practitioner's veins, imbuing that creature with innate mystical power from a distant ancestor. Likewise, the sorcerer may have been born with an uncanny ability to tap into a primordial reservoir of magical energy from somewhere else, such as a celestial body or a cosmic event. Regardless of where they derive their power, sorcerers use the intangible force much like a sculptor uses his hands and chosen medium to give life to a unique creation. Their magic rarely follows any set rules. Instead, they weave the ephemeral matter into something entirely their own. Sorcerers know no limits other than the boundaries of their imagination and mental stamina. Even when they would normally exhaust their arsenal of spells for the day, these ingenious mystical artists can dig down and tap into their reserves to fuel or significantly alter the fabric of their next incantation.

Metoctli

This sorcerer's innate magic comes from his bond to the maguey plant and the beverage distilled from its fermented sap known as pulque. Some observers even believe pulque flows through his veins. The sacred yet alcoholic drink inspires the imbiber to new heights, increasing his drive and enthusiasm as well as his spontaneity. Pulque is the key ingredient for the metoctli's unique abilities. He can transform the ordinary liquid into a magical elixir, use it as a medium to merge souls with another creature, or spread its intoxicating effects to other creatures. Although pulque is most commonly associated with the Aztlis, other humanoid races, most notably dwarves and halflings, disproportionately account for a high percentage of their total numbers.

Pulque Affinity. **(Ex)** Your affinity for pulque grants you Knowledge (Nature) as a class skill, and it allows you to learn cantrips and spells from the druid spell list. When you learn or replace a sorcerer spell of 1st level or higher, you can choose the new cantrip or spell from the druid spell list, treating the spell as one level higher than it typically is, or any spell from the sorcerer spell list. When you cast the druid spell, a flask of pulque must be consumed as an additional material component for the cantrip or spell. You must otherwise obey the restrictions for selecting the spell, and it becomes a sorcerer spell for you. This ability replaces the bloodline power and arcana gained at 1st level.

Nectar of the Gods. **(Su)** At 7th level, you perfect the ability to transform a vial of ordinary pulque into magical elixirs. You can use a swift action to turn the fermented sap of the maguey plant into any magical potion of a 1st level spell that you choose. When you reach 12th level in this class, you can transform pulque into any magical potion of a 2nd level spell that you choose, and at 18th level in this class, you can turn it into any magical potion of a 3rd level spell that you choose. If the potion is not consumed by the end of your next turn, it loses its magical properties and reverts to its original form as ordinary pulque. You may use this ability once per day. This ability replaces the bloodline feat gained at 7th level.

Pulque Haze. **(Sp)** At 15th level, you can attempt to possess another creature. If you have a vial or flask of pulque on your person, you can cast *magic jar* as a spell-like ability. The container of pulque serves as the spell's material component. In addition, maguey leaves sprout from your feet and

completely encase your body in a husk, granting you DR/magic equal to your Sorcerer level. You may use this ability once per day. This ability replaces the bloodline power gained at 15th level.

Out of Mind. **(Su)** At 19th level, your extreme tolerance of pulque makes you immune to poison and the sickened condition. In addition, as a standard action, you can emit an aura of intoxication to a distance of 60 feet. For one minute or until you lose your concentration (as if you were casting a concentration spell), each hostile creature that starts its turn in this aura must succeed on a Fortitude saving throw where the DC is equal to 10 + half your Sorcerer level + your Charisma modifier or become confused (as the *confusion* spell) until the aura ends. A creature who succeeds on its Fortitude saving throw is immune to your aura for 24 hours. Creatures immune to poison damage or the sickened condition are also immune to your aura. You may use this ability a number of times per day equal to 3 + your Charisma modifier. This ability replaces the bloodline feat gained at 19th level.

TONALPOCHQUI

This sorcerer's innate magic comes from his connection to the powers of fate and fortune. He may hail from a line of soothsayers or astronomers who prognosticated future events or descend from a person who exhibited incredibly good or disastrously bad luck throughout his lifetime. The tonalpochqui envisions fate as a malleable force under the right circumstances. Fortune is something to be made or unmade rather than predetermined. These sorcerers weave their magic to gain insight or alter the outcomes of current and future events. The origin is especially popular among the Aztlis who have a propensity for superstitions and fortunetelling.

Divining the Future. **(Ex)** Your connection to the whims of fortune allows you to learn divination cantrips and spells from other classes. When you learn or replace a sorcerer spell of 1st level or higher, you can choose a new divination cantrip or spell from the cleric spell list, treating the spell as one level higher than it typically is, or any other spell from the sorcerer spell list. You must otherwise obey the restrictions for selecting the spell, and it becomes a sorcerer spell for you. This ability replaces the bloodline power and arcana gained at 1st level.

Brief Glimpses. **(Su)** Starting at 1st level, you can see fleeting images of the future. As a swift action, you may try to predict the actions of an enemy you can see within 30 feet of you. When you do so, record the trigger as if you were taking a Ready action. The trigger must correlate to a specific creature you designate at the time you use this feature. Examples include "If the goblin chieftain attacks me or a companion," or "If the goblin shaman casts a spell." You cannot say, "If a goblin steps onto the bridge" if there is more than one goblin present unless the goblin you specifically choose takes the action. Unlike the Ready action, you do not state your response to the trigger. Instead, when the trigger occurs, you may use your action immediately after the triggering action to cast a spell with a casting time of 1 action or shorter targeting the creature that triggered your reaction. If the trigger does not occur before the beginning of your next turn, the attempt is lost.

You can use this feature a number of times per day equal to your Charisma modifier. This ability replaces eschew materials.

Disrupt Magic. **(Su)** At 9th level, you can see wisps of mystical energy in the air that allow you to prognosticate and thwart magic cast by other creatures. When a creature you can see within 30 feet of you casts a spell of 1st level or higher, you can use your immediate action to potentially interrupt the spellcasting process by expending a spell slot one level higher than the spell being cast. When you do so, make a caster level check. The DC equals 10 + double the spell's level. On a success, the creature's spell has no effect. This ability replaces the bloodline power gained at 9th level.

Shape Fortune. **(Su)** At 15th level, you not only can peer into the future, you also can alter it. Whenever you or a companion you can see within 10 feet of you makes an attack roll, saving throw, ability check, skill check, or rolls damage dice, you can use your immediate action and expend a 4th level or higher spell slot to reroll any number of those dice once. This ability replaces the bloodline power gained at 15th level.

One More Time. **(Su)** At 20th level, some events feel as if you had previously witnessed them unfold. When you roll a critical success on any d20 roll during another creature's turn, you can expend a 7th level or higher spell slot and immediately take an extra turn, interrupting the current turn. You may use this ability once per day. This ability replaces the bloodline power gained at 20th level.

WIZARD ARCHETYPES

Academia is a lifelong pursuit. Youngsters blessed with a keen mind and boundless curiosity dive headfirst into their studies, voraciously reading dusty, old tomes with the zeal of a hungry scavenger. Students with an aptitude for magic begin the long journey down the road to becoming a wizard. These practitioners of arcane incantations follow a structured curriculum focused on understanding and memorizing the words and symbols empowering their potent and diverse brand of magic. Consistent with their emphasis on observing formalities, wizards frequently lack the spontaneity found in other spellcasting classes. However, their improved versatility more than compensates for their inability to adjust or modify their spells on the fly. Wizards compile their mystical knowledge into a spellbook that grants them access to a greater number of spells than other classes. Those individuals who have the prerequisite expertise can memorize any spell transcribed onto its pages for future casting. Throughout their careers, wizards undergo a rigorous, well-rounded education, though this dynamic changes as the apprentice prepares to set foot into the real world. A wizard ready to wield more advanced spells must ultimately follow an arcane tradition through study in a specialized field of magic most often associated with a figurative or literal school of magic.

BLOOD MAGE

In Tehuatl, deities frequently demand blood. While it is well established that the blood of living can appease the gods, a small yet growing school of wizards has also discovered that spells written with the life-giving substance also exhibit previously unknown special properties. Unfortunately for the practitioners of this form of magic, only drops of their own blood grant them their unusual powers. Mastering the technique of writing and drawing blood from your own veins proves exceptionally taxing when compared to penning incantations with even the most expensive ink. Tehuatl's residents generally shun and fear wizards who partake in blood magic.

Bloody Spellbook. **(Ex)** At 1st level, you master the techniques of using your own blood to transcribe your incantations into your spellbook. The Bloody Spellbook feature functions the same as the wizard's spellbook with the following exceptions. Because you draw upon a portion of your own lifeforce to empower the book's pages, your reduce your starting hit points by 1 (minimum one) and decreases by 1 again (minimum one) whenever you gain a level in this class. Copying a wizard spell of 1st level or higher into your spellbook takes twice as long to do and costs twice as much. In addition, you take 1 damage for each level of the spell. The transcription attempt fails and all time and money are lost if you avoid or mitigate taking the preceding damage. This ability replaces arcane bond.

Blood Thirst. **(Su)** At 1st level, your spilt blood fuels your magic. Add your Intelligence modifier to the damage you deal with a wizard spell of 1st level or higher targeting one or more creatures with blood in their bodies. If your spell reduces one or more targets to 0 hit points or less, you gain temporary hit points equal to twice the level of the wizard spell. This ability replaces arcane school.

Blood Weapon. **(Ex)** At 1st level, you gain proficiency with a simple or martial piercing or slashing weapon of your choice. This ability alters weapon proficiency.

Blood Offering. **(Su)** At 1st level, your spilt blood can empower your magic. If you have a sharp or pointed object in your hand, you may use your swift action to inflict a minor wound to yourself sufficient to draw blood but not severe enough to deal damage. When you do so, you gain a +1 bonus to your attack rolls with spells until the end of your turn. This bonus increases by +1 for every five wizard levels you possess. You can use this feature a number of times per day equal to 3 + your Intelligence modifier.

Raining Blood. **(Su)** At 6th level, you can spray your enemies with foul blood. When you cast a wizard spell of 1st level or higher with a casting time of 1 action or less, you can use your swift action before the end of your turn to cause bloody globules to fill a 20-foot-radius sphere centered on you. Creatures other than you within the area who have blood in their bodies must succeed on a Fortitude saving throw where the DC is equal to 10 + half your Wizard level + your Intelligence modifier or take 1d6 points of damage per wizard level you possess and become sickened by the tainted blood. Creatures who succeed on the Fortitude saving throw take half as much damage and are not sickened. Because you must expend some of your own blood to fuel this feature, you take 1d6 damage. You can use this ability once per day.

Bloody Sacrifice. **(Su)** At 15th level, you can banish a creature into the realm of its darkest nightmares. When you cast a wizard spell of 1st level or higher with a casting time of 1 action or less, you can use your swift action before the end of your turn to choose a creature with blood in its body that you can see within 60 feet of you. The creature must succeed on a Will saving throw where the DC is equal to 10 + half your Wizard level + your Intelligence modifier. On a failed save, the creature imagines it is restrained atop a sacrificial altar waiting for you to remove its beating heart. The illusion lasts for one minute or until your concentration is broken (as if you were concentrating on a spell). The effect ends early if the creature takes any damage.

The creature is helpless while in this state and has no awareness of its present surroundings. Instead, it only sees and hears you, itself, and the illusory scenery you create. An observer who succeeds on a Sense Motive check against the DC notices that the creature's facial expressions and glassy eyes suggest it is experiencing a terrifying vision in its own mind and appears oblivious to its surroundings. You may use this ability once per day. This ability replaces the bonus feat gained at 15th level.

PIGMENT MAGE

This wizard tradition draws power from color. Its practitioners use a spectrum of hues and specialized pigments to transcribe incantations into their spellbooks. While more expensive and time consuming than copying spells in the conventional manner, these wizards colloquially known as paint wizards believe the extra effort is worth the additional cost. They can use their strange brand of magic to infuse added mystical energy into their spells to inflict various types of extra damage corresponding to an appropriate color. The Poqozas display an odd affinity for this brand of magic, a fact they attribute to their elvish heritage.

Colorful Spellbook. **(Ex)** At 1st level, you discover the ability to use color to enhance your magic. The Colorful Spellbook feature functions the same as the wizard's spellbook with the following exceptions. Copying a spell into your spellbook takes twice as long to do and costs twice as much as normal. When you transcribe a spell into your spellbook, choose one of the following colors to use to record the incantation: blue, green, orange, purple, red, or yellow. Each pigment corresponds with the following damage types.

TABLE C-4: PIGMENT DAMAGE TYPE

Pigment	Damage Type
Blue	Cold
Green	Acid
Orange	Force
Purple	Negative Energy
Red	Fire
Yellow	Electricity

This ability replaces arcane bond.

Pigmentation. **(Su)** Starting at 1st level, you can infuse your pigments into your spells. When you cast a wizard spell of 1st level or higher that targets one creature or object, the spell deals extra damage to the target equal to your Intelligence modifier. The type of damage corresponds with the colored pigment used to transcribe the spell in your spellbook. The damage bonus applies to one damage roll of a spell, not multiple rolls. This ability replaces arcane school.

Expanded Pigmentation. **(Su)** At 6th level, when you cast a wizard spell of 1st level or higher that targets two or more creatures or objects, you can apply the damage from your Pigmentation feature to all targets.

Area Pigmentation. **(Su)** Beginning at 10th level, when you cast a wizard spell of 1st level or higher that affects an area, your Pigmentation feature affects all creatures and objects in the area.

Destructive Pigmentation. **(Su)** At 14th level, you can convert the mystical power stored in your spells. When you cast a wizard spell of 3rd level or higher that targets an area or one or more creatures or objects, the spell may be immediately and permanently erased from your spellbook.

When you do so, your Pigmentation feature generates a pool of extra damage of the corresponding types equal to 1d6 per caster level. You may distribute the damage as you see fit among the affected creatures or objects, though you cannot apply more than half of the total damage to a single target. Any unused extra damage is lost. You may use this ability once per day.

New Spells

The compulsion to create and innovate flows through the fiber of nearly every sentient being born and raised in Tehuatl. While most express themselves through mundane mediums such as painting, song, sculpture, and dance, some steer their imaginations toward the mystical arts. These practitioners devise new cantrips and incantations ideally suited for their unique environment. Their ingenuity appears in the new spells presented in this chapter.

Aura of Altruism

School conjuration (healing); **Level** cleric / oracle 2, paladin 1
Casting Time 1 standard action
Components V, S
Range 30 ft.
Area 30-ft. radius centered on you
Duration concentration, up to 1 min. (D)
Saving Throw Will negates (harmless); **Spell Resistance** yes (harmless)

Cooperative energy radiates from you in an aura with a 30-foot radius. Until the spell ends, the aura moves with you, centered on you. Each nonhostile creature in the aura (including you) can use a swift action to stabilize a living creature that has –1 or fewer hit points within 5 ft. of them and set the creature's current hit points to -1. If the creature later takes damage, it continues dying normally.

Babble

School illusion (figment); **Level** bard 1, mesmerist 1, witch 1
Casting Time 1 standard action
Components V, S
Range short
Target a creature within range
Duration 1 round / level (D)
Saving Throw Will negates; **Spell Resistance** yes

A creature of your choice that you can see within range finds it impossible to communicate verbally or in writing if this spell affects it. The target must succeed on a Will saving throw or any words it speaks or writes come out garbled and incomprehensible. The target is unaware of the spell's effect, as it hears and sees its own words as it intended to say or write them. The target has a -4 penalty on ability checks that rely on speech or writing. The target finds it impossible to cast spells with a verbal component or transcribe any documents including spell scrolls and spells. Anyone listening to the target or reading its written words cannot understand what it is trying to say. Even spells such as *comprehend languages* and *tongues* cannot translate the target's words, as it communicates with nonsensical sounds and indecipherable symbols instead of a different language. At the end of each of its turns, the target can make another Will saving throw. On a success, the spell ends.

Black Hole

School conjuration (creation); **Level** druid 7, psychic 7, shaman 7, sorcerer / wizard 7, witch 7
Casting Time 1 standard action
Components V, S, M (a lodestone)
Range long
Area 100-ft.-radius spread
Duration concentration, up to 1 min. (D)
Saving Throw Fort partial; **Spell Resistance** no

You create a tiny yet immensely dense object to instantly appear at a point that you can see within range. For the duration, the object known as a black hole exerts its enormous gravitational pull in a 100-foot-radius sphere centered on that point. Unsecured objects and secured objects weighing less than 2,000 pounds within the sphere automatically move in a straight line to the closest unoccupied space adjacent to the black hole. The area within the sphere becomes a lightless and soundproof vacuum. If any of the spell's area overlaps with an area of light created by a spell of 7th level or lower, the spell that created the light is dispelled. No sound can be created within or pass through the sphere, making creatures and objects entirely inside the sphere immune to sonic damage. Creatures are deafened while entirely inside the sphere and casting a spell that includes a verbal component is impossible. Creatures required to breathe must hold their breath while inside the sphere. All ranged attacks, including magical ranged attacks, passing through or originating within the sphere automatically miss.

When a creature enters the affected area for the first time on a turn or starts its turn there, it must succeed on a Fortitude saving throw or it is grappled and instantly pulled in a straight line into the closest unoccupied space adjacent to the black hole. At the beginning of its turn, a creature grappled by the black hole takes 4d6 force damage from the gravitational forces pulling it closer to the sphere's center. A creature grappled by the black hole can use its action to make a combat maneuver check against the *black hole*'s CMD. The CMD of *black hole*, for the purposes of escaping the grapple, is equal to 15 + your caster level + your casting stat's modifier. On a success, the creature is no longer grappled.

Bumble

School transmutation; **Level** bard 0, mesmerist 0, sorcerer / wizard 0, witch 0
Casting Time immediate action
Components V, S, M (a drop of oil)
Range short
Target a creature within range attempting to interact with an object
Duration Instantaneous
Saving Throw Reflex negates; **Spell Resistance** yes

A creature of your choice that you can see within range must succeed on a Reflex saving throw or its initial attempt to interact with an object fails, as if the attempt never happened. If the target used an action to interact with the object, the action is lost. The target cannot attempt to interact with the same object again until the end of your next turn. This spell affects only a creature's first attempt to interact with an object rather than end an existing interaction. For instance, the spell can prevent the target from drawing a weapon from its sheath or picking a weapon up from the ground, but it cannot cause the target to drop a weapon it is holding in its hand.

Chinampa

School conjuration (creation); **Level** druid 5, ranger 3, shaman 5
Casting Time 1 standard action
Components V, S, M (a lump of clay)
Range medium
Area 64 five-foot squares
Duration 1 hour, see text (D)
Saving Throw Reflex partial (harmless); **Spell Resistance** no

You create a one-foot-thick parcel of solid, dry land that springs into existence atop up to 1,600 square feet of water (an area 40 feet square, or 64 five-foot squares, or 16 10-foot squares). Each square must have at least one face adjacent to the face of another square. The parcel of land you create consists of bare earth devoid of any vegetation or life. The chinampa cannot cover any existing landmass at or above the water's surface, though you can incorporate any existing landmasses into the parcel you create.

If a creature is partially submerged beneath the water when the land appears, it must succeed on a Reflex saving throw to emerge atop the dry land if it so chooses. On a failed Reflex saving throw, the creature is pushed into the water beneath the dry land. The create can voluntarily sink beneath the water's surface without attempting a Reflex saving throw.

The land has the stability to support the weight of any creatures atop it, though structures made from stone or other heavy materials cause the ground directly beneath it to sink underneath the water's surface until it settles on the bottom. The land is an object that can be damaged and thus destroyed. Each square has hardness 8 and 10 hit points per inch of thickness. Reducing a square to 0 hit points destroys it, causing the soil to break apart and sink to the bottom.

If you maintain your concentration on this spell for the whole duration, the land becomes permanent and cannot be dispelled. The land retains its stability subject to the previously mentioned limitations, but is still subject to natural forces, such as erosion or flooding that may erode or inundate it. Otherwise, the land disappears when the spell ends.

COMPULSIVE STEP

School enchantment (charm) [mind-affecting]; **Level** bard 0, mesmerist 0, sorcerer / wizard 0, witch 0
Casting Time 1 standard action
Components V, S
Range short
Target a creature within range
Duration Instantaneous
Saving Throw Will negates; **Spell Resistance** yes

A creature of your choice that can see and hear you within range can be directed to take a wayward step. You and the target must share a common language. When the spell is cast, you force the target to move five feet into a space of your choosing immediately. This movement does not provoke attacks of opportunity. The creature cannot be forced to move into a space with an obviously deadly hazard such as a chasm or open flames.

COUNTERATTACK

School divination; **Level** bard 1, bloodrager 1, cleric / oracle 1, druid 1, magus 1, ranger 1, shaman 1
Casting Time 1 standard action
Components V, S
Range touch
Target a willing creature
Duration 1 minute or until discharged
Saving Throw Will negates (harmless); **Spell Resistance** yes (harmless)

You touch a willing creature. Once before the spell ends, the target can use its immediate action to make a melee attack against an opponent within reach that missed the target with a melee attack. The target's counterattack must take place immediately after the missed melee attack. The spell then ends.

CREATE BLOOD

School conjuration (creation); **Level** alchemist 1, cleric / oracle 1, psychic 1, sorcerer / wizard 1, witch 1
Casting Time 1 standard action
Components V, S, M (a drop of your blood)
Range short
Area 10-ft.-radius spread or an open container
Duration Instantaneous
Saving Throw Will partial; **Spell Resistance** no

You create 10 gallons of blood within range in an open container. Alternatively, the blood splashes onto all creatures and objects in a 10-ft.-radius spread within range. The blood extinguishes exposed flames in the area and is identical in composition to your own blood. Each creature within the area must succeed on a Will saving throw or drop whatever it is holding and cannot willingly move closer to you and averts its eyes from you, preventing it from seeing you. Creatures that are immune to fear are still doused in blood but are otherwise not affected by this spell.

CREMATION

School necromancy; **Level** cleric / oracle 1, inquisitor 1, medium 1, occultist 1, paladin 1, witch 1
Casting Time 1 standard action
Components V, S, M (a piece of kindling)
Range touch

Target a corpse
Duration Instantaneous
Saving Throw no; **Spell Resistance** no

You touch a corpse or other remains. The target is instantly reduced to a pile of fine, gray dust that cannot be turned into an undead. The creature can be restored to life only by means of a *true resurrection* or a *wish* spell. If it is restored to life, the creature can later be turned into an undead.

DANCE MIQUIZTLI

School enchantment (compulsion) [mind-affecting]; **Level** bard 3, mesmerist 3, sorcerer / wizard 5, witch 5
Casting Time 1 standard action
Components V, S, M (a bone rattle)
Range 60 ft.
Target up to 12 creatures within range
Duration 1 minute
Saving Throw Will negates; **Spell Resistance** yes

You magically compel up to 12 creatures of your choice that you can see within range to perform a frenetic dance routine. Each target must succeed on a Will saving throw or feel an irresistible need to dance. During its turn, the target must use all its movement, even if the target can move back and forth only within the same two spaces. The target incorporates the dance's violent, pounding motions into its movement, causing it to take 1d4 bludgeoning damage for every five feet it travels. If it is impossible for the target to move because of other creatures, objects, or obviously deadly hazards such as a chasm, the target dances in place, becoming flat-footed to attack rolls against it. The target otherwise acts normally. If you or any of your companions damage a creature affected by this spell, the spell ends for that creature. At the end of each of its turns, the target can make another Will saving throw. On a success, the spell's effect ends for the target.

DETECT CORPSE

School divination; **Level** alchemist 1, cleric / oracle 1, inquisitor 1, medium 1, paladin 1, psychic 1, shaman 1, sorcerer / wizard 1, spiritualist 1
Casting Time 1 standard action
Components V, S, M (earth from a grave)
Range 60 ft.
Area cone-shaped emanation
Duration concentration, up to 1 minute/ level (D)
Saving Throw none; **Spell Resistance** no

For the duration, you can sense the presence and location of humanoid corpses and bones that are not undead within 30 feet of you. The spell can penetrate most barriers, but it is blocked by one foot of stone, one inch of common metal, a thin sheet of lead, or 10 feet of wood or dirt.

The amount of information revealed depends on how long you study a particular area.

1st Round: Presence or absence of corpses.
2nd Round: Number and locations of corpses.
3rd Round: You also identify the decedent's race and gender in each case.

FALLING LOGS

School conjuration (creation); **Level** druid 3, shaman 3, sorcerer / wizard 3
Casting Time 1 standard action
Components V, S, M (a splinter of wood)
Range medium
Area 40-ft.-radius spread
Duration Instantaneous
Saving Throw Reflex partial; **Spell Resistance** no

Three vertical 10-foot-long, five-foot-diameter logs appear in individual spaces of your choosing in the air within a 40-foot radius, centered on a point you can see that is 50 feet above the ground. The spell fails if you cannot see a point in the air where the logs could appear (for example, if you are in a room with a low ceiling). The logs must be at least 10 feet apart from one another. The logs simultaneously fall 50 feet to the ground in a straight, vertical line. A creature directly beneath a log must succeed on a Reflex saving throw or take 1d6 points of bludgeoning damage per caster level, fall to the ground prone, and be stunned. On a successful saving throw, the creature takes half as much damage, remains standing, and is not stunned. Each creature within five feet of the point where the log fell, except the creature struck, must succeed on a Reflex saving throw or be knocked prone. The point where the log fell and a random space within five feet of that point then become difficult terrain. At the end of each of its turns, a stunned creature can make a Fortitude saving throw. On a success, the creature is no longer stunned.

FLAY SKIN

School necromancy; **Level** cleric / oracle 3, inquisitor 2, occultist 2, sorcerer / wizard 3, witch 3
Casting Time 1 standard action
Components V, S, M (an obsidian chip)
Range short
Target a creature other than an undead or construct
Duration Instantaneous
Saving Throw Fort partial; **Spell Resistance** yes

Choose a creature other than an undead or construct you can see within range. The target must succeed on a Fortitude saving throw or take 1d6 points of slashing damage per caster level and have portions of its skin flayed from its body. On a successful save, the creature takes half as much damage and its skin is not flayed. Creatures with flayed skin that have natural armor have their natural armor bonus reduced by 2. In addition, creatures with flayed skin become vulnerable to acid, cold, electricity, and fire damage. A creature can take a standard action to repair the flayed skin with a successful Heal check against the DC of the spell. The skin also mends itself if the target receives magical healing.

FLESH TO MAIZE

School transmutation (polymorph); **Level** druid 6, shaman 6, sorcerer / wizard 6, witch 6
Casting Time 1 standard action
Components V, S, M (an ear of maize)
Range medium
Target one creature
Duration Permanent (D)
Saving Throw Fortitude negates; **Spell Resistance** yes

You attempt to turn one creature that you can see within range into the form of a maize plant, though it retains its creature type throughout the metamorphosis. If the target's body is made of flesh, the creature must succeed on a Fortitude saving throw or the target drops everything it is holding and its flesh begins to transform into fibrous plant material. Its legs start to turn into roots and a lower stem; its torso into a central stalk; its arms into leaves; and its head into an ear of maize. On a successful save, the creature is not affected.

A target transformed in this manner has the following traits. The target is unconscious, and it automatically fails all saving throws. Attack rolls against the creature hit against AC 5. The target is unaware of its surroundings. It continues to age and is wholly dependent upon sunlight and water for nourishment. Its roots burrow into any suitable material beneath it, making the creature immune to the prone condition if it is on a suitable surface when transformed. A creature transformed while atop any solid surface such as wood or stone stands in place, though it may still be knocked prone. The creature's gear melds into its new form, but it cannot activate, use, wield, or otherwise benefit from any of its equipment.

FLORAL BOUQUET

School conjuration (creation); **Level** bard 2, cleric / oracle 2, druid 2, ranger 1
Casting Time 1 standard action
Components V, S, M (a flower bulb)
Range medium
Area 20-foot-radius spread
Duration Instantaneous
Saving Throw Fortitude negates; **Spell Resistance** no

A flower bulb streaks from your pointing finger to a point you choose within range and then bursts open to release floral aromas and pungent scents. Each creature in a 20-foot-radius spread centered on that point must succeed on a Fortitude saving throw or be stunned by the sensory overload. A creature that has the *scent* special ability has a -4 penalty on its saving throw. At the end of each of its turns, a stunned creature can make another Fortitude saving throw. Creatures with the *scent* special ability still suffer a -4 penalty on this saving throw. On a success, the creature is no longer stunned.

FORESHADOW

School divination; **Level** cleric / oracle 0, druid 0, psychic 0, shaman 0
Casting Time 1 standard action
Components V, S
Range touch
Target a willing creature
Duration 1 minute or until discharged
Saving Throw Will negates (harmless); **Spell Resistance** yes (harmless)

You touch one willing creature. Once before the spell ends, the target can use its immediate action to move up to half its speed without provoking attacks of opportunity whenever an enemy ends its turn within five feet of the target. The spell ends immediately after the target takes this movement.

HEAT STONE

School evocation (earth, fire); **Level** druid 2, ranger 2, shaman 2
Casting Time 1 standard action
Components V, S, M (a piece of flint)
Range medium
Area 10-ft.-radius spread
Duration 1 round / level (D)
Saving Throw Reflex partial; **Spell Resistance** yes

A contiguous stone surface in up to a 10-foot-radius spread centered on a point within range instantly becomes searing hot. When a creature comes into contact with the affected surface for the first time on a turn or starts its turn in contact with the stone, the creature must succeed on a Reflex saving throw or take 4d6 fire damage. A creature who succeeds on its Reflex saving throw takes half as much damage. Despite the stone's warm temperature, it radiates little heat and shows no outward signs of being hazardous. A creature senses the surface's heat by succeeding on a Perception check against your spell's DC.

INSTILL MADNESS

School enchantment (compulsion) [mind-affecting]; **Level** bard 2, bloodrager 1, mesmerist 2, sorcerer / wizard 3, witch 3
Casting Time 1 standard action
Components V, S
Range medium
Targets a creature in range
Duration 1 round / level
Saving Throw Will negates; **Spell Resistance** yes

One humanoid of your choice that you can see within range must succeed on a Will saving throw or succumb to madness for the duration. While in the throes of madness, the target is no longer an ally, companion, or nonhostile creature toward any another creature for the purpose of determining whether ongoing or new spells and effects affect the target. While mad, the target cannot take swift actions, immediate actions, or attacks of opportunity and only can move or take the attack action. It cannot use or activate magic items, interact with objects it is not already holding, or use any class features unless those features aid its movement or attacks. The madness instantly breaks its concentration, and also causes the target to have a -4 penalty on Charisma, Intelligence, and Wisdom checks and Will saving throws, including those to end this spell.

The target is free to decide whether to move or attack, but when it does so, it acts randomly. If the target moves, it uses all its movement to move in a random direction until it completes its movement or another creature, obstacle, or obviously deadly hazard blocks its path. To determine the direction, roll a d8 and assign a direction to each die face. The target can attack only with natural weapons or any weapon it held when it succumbed to its madness. If the target makes a melee attack, it attacks a random creature within its reach. If the target makes a ranged attack, it targets a random creature it can see within range. The target continues to attack random creatures until another creature it can see hits it with an attack. The target then attacks that creature until the spell ends. If more than one creature hits the target, the target randomly determines which creature it attacks.

At the end of each of its turns, an affected target can make a Will saving throw. If it succeeds, this effect ends for that target.

JAGUAR SPIRIT

School conjuration (summoning); **Level** cleric / oracle 3, druid 3, medium 3, psychic 3, ranger 2, spiritualist 3, summoner / unchained summoner 3, witch 3
Casting Time swift action
Components V, S, M (a jaguar tooth)
Range close
Effect one spectral jaguar
Duration 1 round / level (D)
Saving Throw none; **Spell Resistance** no

You conjure into existence a floating, spectral jaguar that appears within range and lasts for the whole duration. When you cast the spell, you can make a melee touch attack against a creature within five feet of the jaguar using your casting stat in place of strength and your caster level as your base attack bonus. On a hit, the target takes 3d6 force damage and is grappled (escape DC equals your spell's DC). A creature that starts its turn already grappled by the jaguar takes 3d6 force damage. A creature grappled by the *jaguar spirit* can use its action to make a combat maneuver check against the *jaguar spirit*'s CMD. The CMD of *jaguar spirit*, for the purposes of escaping the grapple, is equal to 10 + your caster level + your casting stat's modifier. On a success, the creature is no longer grappled.

As a swift action on your turn, you can move the jaguar up to 40 feet and make an attack against a creature within five feet of it. If the jaguar moves at least 20 feet straight toward a creature right before biting it, the target must succeed on a Fortitude saving throw or be knocked prone.

JINX

School divination; **Level** mesmerist 0, witch 0
Casting Time 1 standard action
Components V, S
Range short
Target a creature within range
Duration 1 minute or until discharged
Saving Throw Will negates; **Spell Resistance** yes

A creature of your choice that you can see within range receives an ominous feeling that something bad is about to happen. The target must succeed on a Will saving throw or be jinxed. On a successful Will saving throw, the target is not affected, and you cannot use this cantrip against it again for 24 hours. Whenever the target rolls a 1 on any d20 roll, including when the target rolls two dice from any effect (such as the fortune or misfortune hexes), the target's turn ends immediately after resolving the outcome from that die roll, if the die roll took place during the target's turn. Regardless of when the die roll occurred, the target cannot take any immediate actions or attacks of opportunity until the beginning of its next turn. The target then has a -2 penalty on attack rolls, saving throws, and ability checks made until the end of its next turn, when the spell ends. A target can be affected by only one *jinx* spell at a time. If you or another creature casts this spell on a target already affected by this spell, the first *jinx* spell immediately ends.

MAGNETIZE

School transmutation; **Level** bard 3, druid 4, shaman 4
Casting Time 1 standard action
Components V, S, M (a small lodestone)
Range medium
Area 40-ft.-radius spread
Duration concentration, up to 1 min. (D)
Saving Throw Fort partial; **Spell Resistance** no

Choose an object made of nickel, iron, cobalt, or an alloy manufactured from any of these metals, such as steel, that you can see within range. The object becomes a powerful magnet attracting all other creatures or objects containing any of the preceding metallic components within a 40-foot-radius spread. Any unsecured objects containing any of the preceding metallic components within the spell's area when it is first cast are pulled in a straight line into the unoccupied space closest to the magnet at the end of your turn.

Ranged weapons and ammunition containing any of the preceding metals or alloys that enter into or originate from within the spell's area automatically miss. When a creature enters the spell's area for the first time or starts its turn there, a creature made from or possessing an object containing any of the preceding metals or alloys must succeed on a Fortitude saving throw. On a failed save, the magnet pulls any handheld objects containing any of the preceding metals or alloys out of the creature's hands, causing them to instantaneously fly through the air in a straight line where they come to rest in the unoccupied space closest to the magnet. A creature made from or wearing objects containing any of the preceding metal components, such as steel armor, are pulled in a straight line 20 feet closer to the magnet, unless its path is blocked by a secured object or another creature. A creature attempting to move away from the magnet must succeed on a Strength check against your spell's DC to do so. On a failed Strength check, the creature cannot attempt to move again until the beginning of its next turn.

NOHPALLI

School conjuration (creation); **Level** cleric / oracle 1, druid 1, shaman 1
Casting Time 1 standard action
Components V, S, M (a cactus needle)
Range medium
Target a creature in range
Duration Instantaneous
Saving Throw no; **Spell Resistance** no

A four-inch-diameter cactus ball with one-inch-long needles streaks toward a target in range. Make a ranged spell attack against the target. On a hit, the target takes 1d8 points of piercing damage per level (max 5d8), and the ball sticks to the target. The target or another creature within five feet of the target can use an action to remove the cactus ball. Unless removed, the target takes 1d8 piercing damage at the end of its next two turns.

NUMB

School illusion (glamer); **Level** cleric / oracle 0, mesmerist 0, psychic 0, sorcerer / wizard 0, witch 0
Casting Time 1 standard action
Components V, S
Range short
Target a creature within range
Duration 1 minute
Saving Throw Will negates; **Spell Resistance** yes

You numb a creature to pain. Choose a creature that you can see within range. The target must succeed on a Will saving throw. On a failed save, the illusion suppresses the target's pain receptors, causing the target to believe its wounds and injuries are harmless scratches requiring no immediate attention. The target never willingly heals itself and refuses assistance from others. When an ally attempts to heal the target, the target resists the spell. At the end of each of the target's turns before the spell ends, the target can make another Will saving throw. On a success, the spell ends. Aztli priests sometimes use this spell on sacrificial victims to ease their suffering.

PALPITATING HEART

School illusion (phantasm) [mind-affecting]; **Level** cleric / oracle 4, psychic 4, sorcerer / wizard 4, spiritualist 3, witch 4
Casting Time 1 standard action
Components V, S, M (a dried animal heart)

Range short
Target a living creature within range
Duration 1 round / 2 levels
Saving Throw Will negates; **Spell Resistance** yes

Choose a creature other than an undead or construct that you can see within range. A spectral hand reaches into that creature's torso and appears to rip out the creature's still-beating heart or other vital organ, which then instantly appears in your hand. Blood and other bodily fluids gush out of the creature's chest. The illusion is perceivable only to you and the target. The target must succeed on a Will saving throw. On a failed save, the target believes the illusion is real, causing it to be stunned for the duration. At the end of each of the target's turns before the spell ends, the target must succeed on a Will saving throw. When it fails its first Will saving throw at the end of its turn, the target becomes unconscious. When it fails the next Will saving throw at the end of its turn, the target drops to -1 hit points and begins dying.

Stunned creatures and unconscious creatures are no longer stunned or unconscious when the spell ends. Dying creatures remain in their current state.

PARASITIC BOND

School necromancy; **Level** sorcerer / wizard 2, witch 2
Casting Time 1 standard action
Components V, S, M (a mosquito larvae)
Range short
Target a creature within range
Duration 1 round / level (max 10)
Saving Throw Fort negates; **Spell Resistance** yes

Choose one creature that you can see within range. The target must succeed on a Fortitude saving throw or take 3d6 damage and become the host for your parasitic bond. On a successful Constitution saving throw, the target takes half as much damage and is not your parasitic host. At the end of each of the host's turns before the spell ends, the host must succeed on a Fortitude saving throw or take 1d6 damage and take 1 Strength damage. Each time the host takes a point of Strength damage from this spell, you gain temporary hit points equal to twice the amount of Strength damage the host has suffered from this spell.

PULQUE INFUSION

School conjuration (creation); **Level** bard 1, druid 1, ranger 1, shaman 1
Casting Time 1 standard action
Components V, S, M (a vial of pulque)
Range short
Target a creature within range
Duration 1 round / level
Saving Throw Fort negates; **Spell Resistance** yes

This spell infuses pulque directly into a creature that you can see within range. It must succeed on a Fortitude saving throw or become sickened. A target automatically succeeds on this saving throw if it cannot be poisoned. The target cannot be frightened while affected by this spell. At the end of each of its turns, the target can make another Fortitude saving throw. On a success, the spell ends on the target.

RUST

School transmutation; **Level** bard 2, druid 2, ranger 1, shaman 2
Casting Time 1 standard action
Components V, S, M (a drop of water)
Range close
Target one object of up to 10 cu. ft. / level or one construct creature of any size
Duration instantaneous
Saving Throw: Will negates (object); **Spell Resistance**: yes (object)

Choose a manufactured object made from iron or an iron alloy, such as steel, that you can see within range. You cause iron oxide (rust) to significantly weaken the object's structural integrity. The object's hardness is reduced by 5, and it gains the fragile quality. Nonmagical weapons affected by this spell crumble into dust when they hit a creature or object, while nonmagical armor and shields affected by the spell disintegrate when an attack hits the creature wearing or holding the protective device. A *make whole* cast on the object repairs the rust damage and restores it to its original state. A magic item or construct made from iron or iron alloy only suffers the hardness reduction and does not gain the fragile quality or crumble to dust from impact.

SLITHER

School transmutation; **Level** sorcerer / wizard 1, witch 1
Casting Time 1 standard action
Components V, S, M (a sloughed snakeskin)
Range touch
Target a creature touched
Duration 1 round / level
Saving Throw: Will negates (harmless); **Spell Resistance**: yes (harmless)

You touch a creature. The touched creature can move full speed while prone, and the target can squeeze through a space that is large enough for a creature two sizes smaller than it. While prone, the target does not suffer penalties on attack rolls or armor class.

STEAM BATH

School conjuration (creation); **Level** cleric / oracle 2, druid 2, magus 2, ranger 1, shaman 2, sorcerer / wizard 2, summoner / unchained summoner 2, witch 2
Casting Time 1 standard action
Components V, S, M (a drop of water and a piece of flint)
Range short
Effect steam spreads in 20-ft. radius, 20 ft. high
Duration 1 min. / level (D)
Saving Throw none; **Spell Resistance** no

You create a 20-foot-radius spread of steam centered on a point within range. The steam obscures all sight, including darkvision, beyond 5 feet. A creature 5 feet away has concealment (attacks have a 20% miss chance). Creatures farther away have total concealment (50% miss chance, and the attacker cannot use sight to locate the target). When a creature enters the spell's area for the first time or starts its turn there, it must succeed on a Reflex saving throw or take 1d6 points of fire damage per caster level (max 10d6). A creature who succeeds on its Reflex saving throw takes half as much damage. The steam lasts for the duration or until a wind of moderate or greater speed (11+ miles per hour) disperses the steam, though the spell instantaneously replaces any dispersed steam if there is a replenishable water source within the spell's area, such as a pond, lake, stream, or river.

STRENGTH IN NUMBERS

School transmutation; **Level** bard 2, cleric / oracle 2, druid 2, psychic 2, ranger 1, shaman 2, sorcerer / wizard 2
Casting Time 1 standard action
Components V, S, M (a strand of spider silk)
Range personal
Duration 1 round
Saving Throw: no; **Spell Resistance**: no

You draw upon the might of others to empower yourself. When you cast this spell, add the combined Strength modifiers (even if it is 0 or a negative number) of up to one companion per 2 caster levels that you can see within 10 feet of you to your own Strength modifier until the end of your next turn. If a companion moves more than 10 feet away from you before this spell ends, you immediately lose that creature's Strength modifier for the whole duration.

Stumble

School divination; **Level** bard 1, mesmerist 1, sorcerer /
wizard 1, witch 1
Casting Time 1 standard action
Components V, S
Range short
Target a creature within range
Duration instantaneous
Saving Throw Reflex negates; **Spell Resistance** yes

A creature of your choice that you can see within range must succeed on
a Reflex saving throw or fall prone. On a successful save, the target is not
affected, and you cannot use this spell against it again for 24 hours.

Superstitious

School enchantment (compulsion) [mind-affecting]; **Level**
mesmerist 0, occultist 0, witch 0
Casting Time 1 standard action
Components V, S
Range short
Target a creature within range
Duration 1 round / level (D)
Saving Throw Will negates; **Spell Resistance** yes

A creature of your choice that you can see within range obsesses over
superstitious rituals if this spell affects it. The target must succeed on a Will
saving throw, or it dwells on real and imaginary omens around it. When the
target misses an attack roll or fails an ability check or saving throw, it takes 1d3
damage. At the end of each of its turns, the target can make another Wisdom
saving throw. On a success, the spell ends.

Time in a Bottle

School transmutation; **Level** psychic 4, sorcerer / wizard 4
Casting Time 1 standard action
Components V
Range personal
Duration 1 round / level or until discharged
Saving Throw: no; **Spell Resistance**: no

You save a brief moment of time for future use. Before the spell ends, you
can use an immediate action to immediately take an extra turn, interrupting the
current turn. When you finish your extra turn, the spell ends.

Triplicate

School illusion (figment); **Level** sorcerer / wizard 3, summoner
/ unchained summoner 2, witch 3
Casting Time 1 standard action
Components V, S
Range short
Effect three illusory duplicates of you
Duration 1 round / level (D)
Saving Throw Will disbelieves; **Spell Resistance** yes

Three illusory duplicates of yourself, which you can use as the origin point
for your spells, appear at unoccupied points you can see within range. Neither
you nor the duplicate can occupy the same space. The duplicates last for
the duration or until you cast this spell again, cast another spell that creates
duplicates of yourself such as *mirror image*, or use an action to dismiss the
illusory duplicates.

The duplicates imitate your actions but remain stationary. As a swift action
on your turn, you can move one of your duplicates up to 20 feet. A duplicate
more than (25 + 5 for every two levels) feet away from you is immediately
destroyed.

Creatures who see you when you cast this spell can track your position
unless you conceal your exact location afterward. Otherwise, a creature who
examines a duplicate can determine it is a duplicate with a successful Will

saving throw. A duplicate's AC equals 10 + your Dexterity modifier. If an
attack hits a duplicate, the duplicate is destroyed. A duplicate can be destroyed
only by an attack that hits it. It ignores all other damage and effects. The spell
ends when all three duplicates are destroyed.

When you cast a spell, you can designate one of your duplicates as the
spell's point of origin, treating it as if it were yourself when determining range,
available targets, and cover for attack rolls. Weapon attack rolls made by a
duplicate automatically miss. You must be able to see the duplicate as well as
any targets and areas the other spell affects. If you cannot do so, the other spell
fails and is lost.

Uncoordinated

School enchantment (compulsion) [mind-affecting]; **Level**
bard 5, druid 6, psychic 6, shaman 6, sorcerer / wizard 6,
witch 6
Casting Time 1 standard action
Components V, S, M (a small strand of copper wire)
Range medium
Target a creature within range
Duration Instantaneous
Saving Throw Reflex partial; **Spell Resistance** yes

You overload the central nervous system of a creature other than a construct
that you can see within range, attempting to disrupt its motor skills. The target
takes 4d6 electricity damage and must succeed on a Reflex saving throw. On
a failed save, the creature's Dexterity score drops to 1. he affected creature
is unable to use Dexterity-based skills, has its speed halved, and it cannot
use immediate actions or take attacks of opportunity. For every five feet
the creature travels, there is a 50% chance the creature moves in a random
direction instead of its intended direction. At the end of 30 days, the creature
can repeat its saving throw against this spell. If it succeeds on its saving throw,
the spell ends.

The subject remains in this state until a heal, limited wish, miracle, or wish
spell is used to cancel the effect of the spell. Creatures immune to electricity
damage are also immune to this spell.

Volcano

School conjuration (creation); **Level** cleric / oracle 8, druid 8,
shaman 8, sorcerer / wizard 8
Casting Time 1 standard action
Components V, S, M (a chunk of volcanic ash)
Range long
Effect an erupting volcano appears
Duration Concentration, up to 1 round / level
Saving Throw Reflex partial, Fortitude partial; **Spell
Resistance** no

Liquid magma from the planet's core surges to the surface, giving rise to a
volcano at a point on the ground that you can see within range. A 60-foot-tall
mound of molten rock and stone with a 10-foot radius centered on the point
you chose instantaneously emerges from the ground. The ground must provide
a firm foundation for the vertical column of rock and stone. If it does not, the
volcano immediately sinks into the earth and the spell has no effect.

If the volcano cuts through a creature's space when it appears, the creature
is pushed to an unoccupied space of its choosing closest to the volcano's
base. If the volcano cuts through a space occupied by an object or structure,
the volcano deals 10 points of bludgeoning and fire damage per level (max
200) to the object or structure and then pushes it into an unoccupied space of
your choosing closest to the volcano. If a structure drops to 0 hit points, it is
torn apart and razed to the ground. A creature within half the distance of the
collapsed structure's height must succeed on a Reflex saving throw or take 8d6
bludgeoning damage, get knocked prone, and be buried in the rubble requiring
a DC 25 Strength check as an action to escape. The DC can be adjusted higher
or lower depending on the building's size and shape as well as its material
components. On a successful save, the creature takes half as much damage and
does not fall prone or become buried.

For the duration, the small yet potent volcano belches pumice, lava, and
pyroclastic gases within a 100-foot-radius sphere centered on the point you
previously chose and causes the ground in the area to become difficult terrain.
When you cast this spell and at the end of each turn you spend concentrating

on it, the falling pumice deals 5d6 bludgeoning damage to each creature and object in the area, while the falling lava deals 8d6 fire damage to each creature and object in the area. A creature who makes a successful Reflex saving throw takes half as much bludgeoning and fire damage. In addition, each creature in the area must also succeed on a Fortitude saving throw or take 4d6 damage and be sickened from the toxic gases. On a successful save, the creature takes half as much damage and is not sickened.

The volcano is an object made of stone that can be damaged and destroyed. It has a 10-foot-radius base and a five-foot-radius opening at its apex, from which its pumice, lava, and toxic gases flow. It has hardness equal to your caster level and each 10-foot-square vertical section has 450 hit points. Reducing a section to 0 hit points destroys it, which causes the precariously balanced volcano to immediately collapse on itself. When this occurs, the volcano no longer deals bludgeoning or fire damage, but the toxic gases seeping through the rubble still deals damage to creatures in the area and sickens them.

WALL OF SMOKE

School evocation [air]; **Level** druid 2, shaman 2, sorcerer / wizard 2, summoner / unchained summoner 2
Casting Time 1 standard action
Components V, S, M (a small lump of coal)
Range medium
Effect wall up to 10 ft. / level long and 5 ft. / level high (S)
Duration 1 round / level
Saving Throw Fortitude partial; see text; **Spell Resistance** yes

You create a 5-foot-thick wall of thick, black smoke on a solid surface within range. The wall is opaque and cannot be dispersed by high winds despite being composed of wispy vapors. It is also difficult terrain.

If the wall cuts through a creature's space when it appears, the creature within its area must succeed on a Fortitude saving throw. On a failed save, a creature takes 1d6 points of acid damage per level (max 10d6) and is blinded by the smoke. The creature takes half as much damage on a successful save and is not blinded. A creature who enters the wall for the first time on a turn or ends its turn there must succeed on a Fortitude saving throw or take 1d6 points of acid damage per level (max 10d6) and be blinded by the smoke. The creature takes half as much damage on a successful save and is not blinded. At the end of each of its turns, a blinded creature can make another Fortitude saving throw. On a success, the creature is no longer blinded.

WAR CRY

School enchantment (charm) [mind-affecting]; **Level** bard 2, mesmerist 2, paladin 1
Casting Time 1 standard action
Components V, S
Range 30 feet
Targets 1 creature / level
Duration 1 round
Saving Throw Will negates (harmless); **Spell Resistance** yes (harmless)

Your war cry whips your allies into a frenzy. Choose up to one creature per caster level within range. When making a melee weapon attack, each target adds your Charisma modifier (minimum of 1) to the damage roll. In addition, each target has DR 5 / —.

WAR DANCE

School enchantment (compulsion) [mind-affecting]; **Level** bard 2, bloodrager 1, inquisitor 2, mesmerist 2, paladin 1
Casting Time 1 standard action
Components V, S, M (a sandal)
Range 60 feet
Targets 1 creature / level
Duration 1 round / level
Saving Throw Will negates (harmless); **Spell Resistance** yes (harmless)

You inspire allies to move in sync with you during battle. Choose up to one creature per caster level that you can see within range. Whenever you move, even if spread across consecutive actions, a target that can see you can use its immediate action to move up to 15 feet in the same pattern and direction as you. You and any targets duplicating your steps move simultaneously. The target can use its immediate action at any point during your movement, but once it starts to duplicate your movements, it must follow the exact same path you do. Its movement ends when it stops following your path or it has moved 15 feet, whichever comes first. For instance, if you move 10 feet north, five feet northeast, and then turn west and move 15 more feet, a target that can see you can move 10 feet north and then five feet northeast, but it cannot move 10 feet north and then move five feet west because it did not trace your exact steps when it skipped your northeast motion.

NEW EQUIPMENT

The people of Tehuatl rarely sit still, physically or mentally. Their intellectual curiosity inspires them to constantly search for knowledge, while their ingenuity allows them to apply their newfound discoveries to aid them in their endeavors. A miniscule handful of technological advances are predominately confined to small corners of the island for various reasons, but the overwhelming majority of groundbreaking inventions spread across Tehuatl at breakneck speeds as local artisans and scholars devise innovative ways to enhance the original creation. The following chapter presents a broad overview of these wondrous devices ranging from armor, weapons, clothing, gear, and, of course magic items.

NEW ARMOR

Steel and heavy armor fare poorly in Tehuatl's humid, semitropical climate. Over time, frequent rainfall and the moisture in the air take a toll on the ferrous metal's durability. Magical equipment ignores the ravages of rust, but being encapsulated within a thick shell of metal on a hot, sticky afternoon under the sun's relentless glare feels like a hellish torment. The island's weather conditions and environment generally lead most warriors to value flexibility and comfort over maximizing protection. Of course, some individuals choose the latter options, most notably the Firebrand dwarves of the Tepepan Mountains, the elves who still prefer chain shirts, and the Tlotls who closely guard the secrets of forging steel. Nonetheless, the bulk of the new armor and shields presented in the following section adheres to the principles of providing lightweight defensive options without compromising stealth and mobility.

LIGHT ARMOR

This defensive equipment typically consists of thin, flexible material stitched together in layers to provide stopping power against projectiles and sharp implements as well as deadening the impact of bludgeoning weapons that strike the armor.

Ichcahuipilli. This two-inch-thick light armor resembles a vest designed to protect the wearer's torso from the neck to the hips against arrows and sharp blades. It consists of layers of cotton and vegetable fiber stitched together in a network of interconnected diamond-shaped patterns and then soaked in brine or another saline solution to harden the materials.

Tlahuiztli. Made from cotton or linen supplemented by hide or leather, this light armor covers the wearer's arms and legs and is worn over the ichcahuipilli. Unlike the basic undercoat, the tlahuiztli almost always boasts elaborate decorative features such as feathers, dyes, and other ornamental accoutrements. The armor's intricate and beautiful designs flaunt the wearer's wealth and status, giving the wearer a +2 circumstance bonus on Diplomacy and Intimidate checks to influence nonhostile Aztlis. The tlahuiztli presented in **Table 3–1** incorporates the underlying ichcahuipilli in its cost, weight, and game statistics.

MEDIUM ARMOR

Protective gear falling into this category provides added defense at the expense of mobility. Supple materials are generally combined with more rigid, durable components to allow the wearer to better fend off attacks while not bogging him down with overly heavy gear.

Cipacahuipilli. This unusual armor follows the basic schematics for creating ichcahuipilli armor with a few modifications. Surprisingly, this medium armor is thinner than its lighter counterpart, but the flat pieces of hide and bone strategically sewn into the fabric adequately compensate for its lesser thickness. The armor's name comes from the flat sections of crocodile vertebrae and hide stitched into the material at vulnerable spots to improve toughness without adding tremendous weight and bulkiness. Most importantly, the armor's lack of metallic pieces or parts makes it immune to rust and suitable for druids.

Olli. Armor smiths combine latex and the juice from a morning glory vine to create a flexible and resilient material resembling modern rubber. Although typically used to create the tlatchli, clever innovators use the durable substance to protect warriors from injury. The lightweight suit includes a jacket and leggings. An inner and outer lining of breathable linen provides added comfort.

KEEP IT SIMPLE OR REALISTIC?

The following sections present new armor and weapons that share many similarities yet have some noteworthy differences from commonly found armor and weapons. You have two options when dealing with the new armor and weapons presented here. You can choose to keep this section simple by retaining the descriptive entries for the armor and weapons while assigning them the same game statistics and costs as existing armor. Alternatively, you can use the costs, game statistics, and special abilities presented below in their entirety. It is recommended that you adopt a consistent approach to handling the armor and weapons rather than treating some items as currently existing armor and weapon types while incorporating the special rules for other items. If you opt for the simple choice, the equivalent existing item appears as the last entry in **Tables 3–1** and **3–2**.

While wearing this armor, you reduce any falling damage you take by 5 points, though you cannot reduce the falling damage below 0. Because it is made from plant-based products, druids are permitted to wear olli, and it is immune to rust. Furthermore, you are not considered to be wearing medium armor against the effects the extreme heat.

HEAVY ARMOR

Those willing to sacrifice mobility and comfort for added protection ultimately turn to heavy armor. This category of defensive equipment covers the entire body with hard, sturdy materials with the strength to deflect projectiles and even powerful blows from a melee weapon.

Ollixalli. One day, Atoyapaca, an innovative botanist and renowned jeweler heated olli and combined it with ground quartz to enhance its strength. His bold experiment exceeded his wildest expectations, leading others to follow in its footsteps by adding other silica-based and sulfurous components to the liquified olli mixture. The delicate and laborious process of creating ollixalli is a tightly guarded secret confined to those who have the technical expertise and specialized equipment required to set the ollixalli mold. Unlike conventional heavy armor, a suit of ollixalli consists of a lightweight jacket and pants that protect the torso and limbs. Ollixalli has no metal components, making it suitable for druids and immune to rust. While wearing ollixalli armor, you are not considered to be wearing heavy armor against the effects of extreme heat. Because of the specialized training and equipment needed to create ollixalli, the armor remains extremely expensive and rare.

NEW WEAPONS

The lack of iron and steel has never hampered the island's weapon designers. The craftsmen who build implements of war emphasize creativity over components. Used properly, wood, stone, and other natural materials can be deadlier than a metal sword. Obsidian, a viciously sharp volcanic glass, takes a prominent role in this arms race. Its edges are keener than any steel blade, allowing the hard, brittle material to slice through flesh and bone with surgical precision. Yet achieving this incredible cutting edge also makes obsidian vulnerable to fracturing when it comes into contact with a hard object. Despite these breakthroughs, some of Tehuatl's inhabitants, most notably the Firebrand dwarves of the Tepepan Mountains, still place their trust in the forge's molten steel.

Atlatl. This easily made wooden device uses javelins for ammunition. To use this javelin launcher, you must place the javelin's butt into a cup, groove, or spur at the top of the atlatl. With your forearm perpendicular to your arm and the atlatl and javelin both parallel to the ground, you let the javelin rest atop your fingers while you hold the atlatl's base in the palm of your hand. When you are ready to release the javelin, you fling your forearm and wrist forward, which in turn pushes the javelin out of your hand toward the intended target.

Table 3–1: Tehuatl Armor

Armor	Cost	Armor Bonus	Max Dexterity Bonus	Armor Check Penalty	Arcane Spell Failure Chance	Speed (30 ft. base)	Weight	Equivalent
Light Armor								
Ichcahuipilli	15 gp	+1	+8	0	5%	30 ft.	4 lbs.	padded
Tlahuiztli	200 gp	+3	+6	-1	15%	30 ft.	6 lbs.	parade armor
Medium Armor								
Cipacahuipilli	35 gp	+4	+4	-3	20%	20 ft.	15 lbs.	hide
Olli	75 gp	+5	+3	-4	25%	20 ft.	12 lbs.	scale mail
Heavy Armor								
Ollixalli	1,000 gp	+8	+0	-7	40%	20 ft.	25 lbs.	half plate

Table 3–2: Tehuatl Weapons

Weapon	Cost	Damage (Medium)	Critical	Range	Weight	Type	Special	Equivalent
Simple Light Melee Weapons								
Itztopilli	4 gp	1d6	x2	—	2 lbs.	S	see text	Handaxe
Tecpatl	2 gp	1d4	x2	—	1 lb.	P or S	fragile, see text	Dagger
Simple Ranged Weapon								
Atlatl	1 sp	1d6	x2	60 ft.	1 lb.	P	—	None
Martial Light Melee Weapons								
Ollitetlacotl	35 gp	1d6	x2	—	1 lb.	B	—	Mace, light
Ollitztli	40 gp	1d6	x2	—	1 lb.	B and P	see text	Morningstar
Martial One-Handed Melee Weapons								
Macuahuitl	10 gp	1d8	x2	—	2 lbs.	S	fragile, see text	Longsword
Martial Two-Handed Melee Weapons								
Tepoztopilli	25 gp	1d10	x3	—	6 lbs.	S	fragile, reach, see text	Glaive

Itztopilli. This axe has a wooden haft with a bronze head fitted into a groove built into the haft. The head is long and narrow, and its cutting surface is only slightly wider than the axe's flat back. The itztopilli's versatile design allows you to hack into flesh as well as chop wood with remarkable accuracy and comparable ease. Indeed, most woodworkers incorporate the weapon into a standard set of carpenter's tools. If you are proficient with the itztopilli, and you made an attack roll with the weapon within the last 24 hours, you also gain a +1 circumstance bonus to Craft (carpentry).

Macuahuitl. Made from hardwood such as oak, this weapon resembles a long, flat paddle with obsidian or flint chips embedded into the weapon's edges. The insertion of these incredibly sharp stones gives the weapon unmatched cutting power at the cost of increased fragility. When you attack a creature with this weapon and roll a 20 on the attack roll, you score a critical hit as normal and deal an extra effect if the attack roll confirms against the target by 10 or more. The creature struck takes 1d8 bleed damage at the start of each of its turns due to the blade gouging a deep laceration through the creature's flesh. The bleed damage increases by 1d8 if you inflict another deep laceration during a subsequent attack.

Ollitetlacotl. This hardened rubber club is difficult to manufacture yet greatly valued among Aztli warriors for its lightweight punching power. Because of its unusual components and unique feel, the weapon requires more skill and training to wield than an ordinary club.

Ollitztli. Almost identical in its size, shape, and general appearance to the ollitetlacotl, this vicious weapon has an important added enhancement over its similar counterpart. When the olli starts to harden yet retains some malleability, the makers embed obsidian slivers into the weapon, riddling its surface with dozens of slightly raised spikes that puncture flesh like fine needles. Unlike the macuahuitl, which uses obsidian chips to form a contiguous edge, only tiny slivers of obsidian protrude above the weapon's surface, giving it a rough texture akin to a vine covered in tiny, fine-yet-rigid needles. Although the weapon lacks the ability to rip through flesh and bone like the macuahuitl, the tiny needles excel at delivering poison to a victim. When you coat this weapon with injury poison and roll a 20 on the attack roll, the creature you hit suffers a -2 penalty on its saving throws against the injury poison.

Tecpatl. Carved from flint or obsidian, this double-edged knife has a pointed tip and a decorative wooden, stone, or mosaic handle. Although an effective, close-quarters combat weapon, the tecpatl is predominately used in religious rites and revered for its multitude of symbolic roles. When used in battle, it may open a deep laceration in the same manner as described under the **macuahuitl** entry (see above).

Tepoztopilli. This polearm has two components: a five- to six-foot-long wooden shaft carved from a single piece of wood and an oblong wooden head attached to the end of the shaft. The head ends in a sharp point, and like the macuahuitl, obsidian fragments are glued into grooves cut into the head to increase its deadly cutting power. When used in battle, it may open a deep laceration as described under the **macuahuitl** entry (see above). However, because such a blow requires greater precision than the macuahuitl, you inflict only a deep laceration when you roll a 20 and confirm against the target by 15 or more.

Adventuring Gear

Like their armor and weaponry, Tehuatl's adventurers capitalize on the ingredients at hand to create potent concoctions and wondrous instruments to give adventurers more than a fighting chance in a dangerous world. These tools of the trade incorporate the designers' understanding of botany, astronomy, mathematics, and other scientific disciplines into these creations.

Table 3–3: Tehuatl Adventuring Gear

Item	Cost	Weight
Cempohualxochi (vial)	50 gp	—
Chilli (vial)	50 gp	—
Coanenepilli (vial)	50 gp	—
Copal glue (flask)	100 gp	1 lb.
Cuitlapan	3 gp	5 lbs.
Ixquichten	250 gp	5 lbs.
Iyollo (vial)	75 gp	—
Kindling sticks	1 cp	1 lb.
Mictlampa	100 gp	1 lb.
Ollicactli	50 gp	—
Ollixima (vial)	25 gp	—
Passiflora (vial)	50 gp	—
Rust dust (vial)	25 gp	—
Tecuaniz (flask)	25 gp	—
Tlilitl (vial)	25 gp	—
Uictli	2 gp	5 lbs.
Xochitl (vial)	25 gp	—
Zoyoyatic (flask)	20 gp	—

Cempohualxochi. A creature that drinks this vial of liquid made from marigold gains a +2 alchemical bonus against death effects for 1 hour.

Chilli. Made from the spiciest peppers on the island, this vial may be used as a food additive to enhance flavor and add heat to a dish when used in small doses — or it can be used to harmful effect. If you add the entire vial to food or liquid, the creature who eats or drinks an item containing chilli must succeed on a DC 10 Fortitude saving throw or be blinded and unable to speak for one minute. Alternatively, as a standard action, you can splash the contents of this vial onto a creature within five feet of you, or you can throw it up to 20 feet to shatter on impact. When you splash the chilli or throw it, make a ranged attack against a target creature, treating the chilli as a splash weapon. A creature struck by chilli must succeed on a DC 10 Fortitude saving throw or be blinded for 1d4 rounds. (A creature struck by chilli can still speak unlike a creature who ingests chilli.) Creatures immune to being poisoned are also immune to chilli.

Coanenepilli. A creature can use a full round action to apply or administer this salve to an injury or wound that dealt ability damage from a poison. If the salve is applied to the target creature before the end of the target's next turn after taking the poison's damage, the target heals 1d4 ability damage. The creature cannot heal more ability damage that it took from the poison's damage during its last turn.

Copal Glue. When mixed, this amalgamation of cooked resin from copal and pine trees creates a strong and durable adhesive. When found, a container of this glue contains 1d6 + 1 ounces of the substance. One ounce of the glue can cover a 1-foot-square surface. It takes 1d4 + 1 rounds to set. You can use the glue to help repair a damaged or broken item. When you use the glue in this manner, you gain a +2 alchemical bonus on the check to repair the object. When applied to a surface that can be opened, such as a door, lid, or gate, the object is more difficult to force open; the DC to pry the object open increases by 1d4 + 1. The bond lasts indefinitely, though once a bonded surface is forced open, or a paired object becomes broken again, the glue is destroyed.

Cuitlapan. Primarily used to carry heavy loads long distances, this device consists of a wooden frame slung over your back. A cord affixed to the frame is then wrapped around your waist to keep the load secure, while a second strap loops just above your forehead for added balance. The cuitlapan has a volume of 1–1/2 cubic feet, and a weight capacity of 50 pounds of gear.

Ixquichten. This book's written pages made from maguey leaves contain mathematical formulas for calculating the length, area, and volume of numerous geometric shapes as well as computing the distances between two or more objects based upon these formulas. Whenever you make a knowledge check pertaining to mathematics or a closely related field such as physics or architecture, you may review the contents of this book for 10 minutes. When you do so, you gain a +2-circumstance bonus to the check. You must conduct a separate review of the book's contents for each skill check.

Iyollo. A creature that drinks this delicious, chocolate-flavored drink experiences exhilaration and euphoria for one hour. Whenever you fail a Will saving throw, you do not suffer the effects from the failed saving throw until the end of your next turn. Until then, you are aware of the failed saving throw's potential consequences and may take actions to counteract its effects. In addition, you have a +2 alchemical bonus on Will saving throws made to end an ongoing spell or effect, when applicable.

Kindling Sticks. Without steel, most people use kindling sticks to start a fire. There are enough sticks in the kit to start 10 fires.

Mictlampa. Icons and symbols cover the face of this flat, round wooden board. The contraption has three movable hands corresponding to fixed points in the sky. When the hands are aligned correctly, it reveals your current position in relation to the four cardinal directions. It takes a successful DC 5 Knowledge (geography) check to correctly align the movable hands and interpret the results.

Ollicactli. These sandals contain rubber padding and soles wrapped between two layers of leather for enhanced durability and cloth for added comfort. The shoes offer protection against the terrain and the elements. While you wear these sandals, you gain a +2-circumsstance bonus on Constitution saving throws made when making a forced march and you gain resist 2 electricity damage.

Ollixami. This vial of black, clay-like material can cover a one-foot-square surface. Made from a mixture of latex, juice from the morning glory vine, and lime juice, it takes 1d4 rounds for this substance to set. You can use the material to create a watertight seal or patch a hole in a canoe, roof, or other surface by forming it in the desired shape before it hardens. The bond can repel water and act as a sealant, but it lacks the adhesive strength to repair a broken object.

Passiflora. A creature that drinks a vial of this liquid made from passion flower has a +2 alchemical bonus on saving throws against being paralyzed for one hour.

Rust Dust. As a standard action, you can spread the contents of this vial onto an unattended manufactured object. The vial contains enough dust to coat a single object measuring one-foot square. If the object is made of a ferrous metal such as iron or steel, the dust chemically reacts with the metal for one minute. When the oxidation process ends, patches of orange rust appear on the object's surface. It gains the broken condition. The dust has no effect on magic items, constructs, or objects currently affected by a spell or magical effect.

Tecuaniz. As a standard action, you can splash the contents of this flask onto a creature within five feet of you, or you can throw it up to 20 feet to shatter on impact. In either case, make a ranged attack against a target creature, treating the tecuaniz as a splash weapon. The flask contains a mixture of herbs that distracts animals. If the target is a beast, it is shaken until the end of its next turn.

Tlilitl. A creature that drinks this vial of vanilla-flavored liquid with hints of chocolate gains a +2 alchemical bonus on saving throws against being put to sleep by magic for one hour.

Uictli. The wedge-shaped wooden or bronze blade attached to the end of this five-foot-long wooden pole is used to burrow into the earth to till, remove, or carve irrigation channels through soil and loose stone. A creature using an uictli has a +2-circumstance bonus on ability and skill checks made to escape being buried, as long as the creature using the tool is not restrained or paralyzed.

Xochitl. A creature that drinks this vial of vanilla-flavored liquid suffers a -2 penalty on saving throws against being put to sleep by magic for 1 hour. Alternatively, a creature who drinks xochitl less than one hour before beginning a night's rest falls into a deep slumber. A creature who normally needs eight hours of sleep awakens refreshed after four hours of sleep, as if it had completed its rest normally.

Zoyoyatic. As a standard action, you can splash the contents of this flask onto a creature within five feet of you, or you can throw it up to 20 feet to shatter on impact. In either case, make a ranged attack against a target creature, treating the zoyoyatic as a splash weapon. The flask contains powder made from the crushed seeds of the sapodilla herb. If the target is a mouse, rat, or wererat, it takes 2d6 acid damage.

MOUNTS AND VEHICLES

Beasts of burden are few and far between in Tehuatl, while wheeled vehicles are merely an oddity. Its people have undertaken little effort to domesticate the wild animals roaming across the island. Despite taming turkeys, ducks, and dogs, none of these creatures has the strength or stamina to haul wagons or carry large loads of goods long distances. Instead of expediting travel across Tehuatl, heavy wagons would constantly get bogged down in mud and standing water. Furthermore, the island's small size in comparison to Akados and Libynos does not create tremendous need or demand for a transportation network stretching across thousands of miles. Instead, commerce centers around the island's numerous waterways, including the Great Canal separating the Aztlis from the Poqozas. While most of Tehuatl's residents haul goods by canoe or by foot when traveling overland, there are some circumstances where people turn to a novel solution. Although not domesticated, the ilhuitecuani, a massive member of the pinniped family, can be used to lug an apanimacal, a hybrid aquatic-land craft across relatively flat and stable ground. The following mount and waterborne vehicles are available throughout Tehuatl:

Acalli. This large vessel made from spruce wood measures 10 feet across and 75 feet in length from its upturned bow to stern. The waterborne vehicle can accommodate a combination of up to 60 passengers or three tons of goods. It takes a crew of six to 10 oarsmen to propel the vessel.

Apanimacal. The apanimacal combines several technologies to create a vehicle suitable for aquatic and land travel. The sleek vehicle is 30 feet long and 10 feet wide with an elevated deck atop its cargo hold and a tapered bow and stern. It can accommodate a combination of up to 20 passengers and 3,000 pounds of goods. It takes a crew of four to operate the vehicle. Its hull is completely flat, which allows it to float on the water or be pulled across the ground as if it were a sled. Some models have a series of ski-like rails that can be attached to the vessel's undercarriage while it is still underwater. The apanimacal is always propelled by an ilhuitecuani tethered to its bow.

Canoe. Carved out of the trunk of a single tree, this waterborne vehicle has an upturned bow and stern and is 15 feet long. It can accommodate three passengers, including its driver, or transport the equivalent weight in goods. The driver propels the vehicle with a long pole or paddle.

Ilhuitecuani. At a weight of nearly 5,000 pounds and almost 20 feet long, the massive ilhuitecuani looks more like a whale than an enormous member of the seal family. This carnivorous wild animal can be temporarily tamed or at least placated with abundant quantities of food — roughly 100 pounds of meat per day — and the proper coaxing. The ilhuitecuani is predominately used to haul the hybrid land-water vehicle known as the **apanimacal** (see above).

TABLE 3-4: MOUNT

Item	Cost	Land Speed	Swim Speed	Carrying Capacity
Ilhuitecuani	175 gp	20 ft.	40 ft.	800 lbs.

TABLE 3-5: WATERBORNE VEHICLES

Item	Cost	Speed
Acalli	4,000 gp	1 mph
Apanimacal	1,500 gp	2 mph on flat land or water
Canoe	150 gp	1–1/2 mph

MAGIC ITEMS

Courage and ingenuity alone can sometimes bring you only so far. When all seems lost, adventurers frequently turn to magic to even the odds and win the day. The sages and scholars who create magic items on Tehuatl frequently enchant readily available objects, items, and materials. The magic items appearing in the following section embody such principles.

ARMOR OF ELUSIVENESS

Aura moderate abjuration; **CL** 7th; **Slot** armor; **Price** 36,000 gp; **Weight** —

Unlike most specific magic armors, the *Armor of Elusiveness* can use ichcahuipilli, hide, leather, olli, ollixalli, studded leather, or tlahuiztli armor as the base armor. Add the cost of the chosen base armor to the cost of this item and use that armor's weight.

Warriors hoping to avoid being captured covet this *+1 slick* armor, which appears to be coated with an oily sheen. While wearing this armor, magic cannot cause you to be paralyzed or restrained. When grappled, you can use a swift action or a standard action, but not both, to escape the grapple via the Escape Artist skill.

Feats Craft Magic Arms and Armor; **Spells** *freedom of movement, grease*; **Price** 18,000 gp

ARROW OF FLESH FINDING

Aura moderate abjuration; **CL** 9th; **Slot** —; **Price** 2,000 gp; **Weight** —

This *+1 arrow* is a magic weapon with the unusual ability to avoid striking inanimate objects in its path. When you make a ranged attack roll with the arrow, the target of your ranged attack does not gain any AC bonus from cover granted by an inanimate object. You can ignore up to 4 points of AC granted by armor or a shield. If the target's body is made of flesh, the arrow deals an extra 3d10 piercing damage on a successful hit. Once an *arrow of flesh finding* hits a target, it becomes a nonmagical arrow.

Feats Craft Magic Arms and Armor; **Spells** *true strike*; **Price** 1,000 gp

BALCHÉ

Aura faint divination; **CL** 3rd; **Slot** —; **Price** 1,000 gp; **Weight** —

This mildly intoxicating concoction is a mixture of tree bark soaked in honey and water. When found, a vial contains 1d4 + 1 one-ounce doses of the fermented liquid. You can use a standard action to drink a dose. The effects last for 10 minutes. When you do so, you gain a greater understanding of nature. You have a +2 alchemical bonus on Knowledge (nature) checks and Charisma checks made when interacting with creatures with the Fey type. While in the outdoors where nature has not been replaced by construction, such as a town or the interior of a building, you ignore difficult terrain and cannot be surprised. When crafted, the vial contains all 5 doses.

Feats Craft Wondrous Item; **Spells** *enhanced diplomacy*; **Price** 500 gp

BOX OF ROCKS

Aura moderate transmutation; **CL** 9th; **Slot** —; **Price** 25,000 gp; **Weight** 1 lb.

This small, rectangular wooden box features decorative mosaic artwork depicting meteors streaking across the heavens on its exterior. It has no latches nor hinges, yet it stays tightly sealed until you speak the command word. While holding the one-pound box, you can use a standard action to speak the box's command word and spill the box's 3d4 pebbles on the ground within 10 feet of you. The pebbles disperse in random spaces within 10 feet of you. Each pebble lands in its own space, but it cannot land in the same space you occupied when you released the pebbles. At the end of your turn, each pebble then instantly fragments into a cloud of tiny rocks that swirl around in a 10-foot-high, five-foot-diameter cylinder in the space where it landed for one minute. A stone cylinder may not occupy the same space as another stone cylinder, though they may occupy the same space as a creature. The cylinders remain in the same space for the duration unless you use a swift action on your turn to move one cylinder up to 20 feet.

When a creature enters a space containing a cylinder of stones for the first time on a turn or starts its turn there, the creature must succeed on a DC 15 Reflex saving throw or take 3d6 bludgeoning damage. The creature must succeed on a Reflex saving throw for each space it enters to avoid taking bludgeoning damage.

The stone cylinders swirl around for one minute before the rock fragments making it up fall harmlessly to the ground. The space where each cylinder falls becomes difficult terrain. Once opened, the box remains open and empty. It does not seal shut again until one minute after the stone cylinders stop swirling. This box can be used 3 times per day.

Feats Craft Wondrous Item; **Spells** *raging rubble*; **Price** 12,500 gp

CHICAHUAZTLI

Aura moderate enchantment; **CL** 9th; **Slot** —; **Price** 12,500 gp; **Weight** 4 lbs.

This staff made from a long bone from a large beast or humanoid can be wielded as a *+1 / +1 quarterstaff*. It allows the use of the following spells:

• *create blood* (1 charge)
• *dance miquiztli* (5 charges)
• *war cry* (2 charges)
• *war dance* (2 charges)

Feats Craft Staff; **Spells** *create blood, dance miquiztli, war cry, war dance*; **Price** 6,250 gp

COCOA BEAN

Aura faint divination; **CL** 3rd; **Slot** —; **Price** 7,500 gp; **Weight** —

This dried and fermented seed from the cocoa tree is usually found in a small pod containing 2d6 cocoa beans. You can use a standard action to eat this seed. When you do so, you heighten your awareness, improve your mood, and gain extra energy for 10 minutes. You have a +2 enhancement bonus on the following die rolls: saving throws against being charmed or frightened, Perception checks, and on rolls for initiative. In addition, your speed gains an enhancement bonus of 10 feet. If you eat two or more beans in an hour, there is a cumulative 25 percent chance for each bean after the first that you gain the fatigued condition at the beginning of your next turn after the bean's effects end. When crafted, a pod contains all 12 beans.

Feats Craft Wondrous Item; **Spells** *haste*; **Price** 3,750 gp

CUACALALATLI OF THE BEAST

Aura faint transmutation; **CL** 7th; **Slot** head; **Price** 16,000 gp; **Weight** 2 lbs.

These wooden helmets are shaped into the likenesses of various beast heads. The protective device fits over your head and covers the top and back of your skull as well as your jawline. While wearing this helmet, you gain its abilities. The type of beast associated with the helmet determines its specific properties.

Crocodile: You discover the reptile's techniques for grabbing and thrashing its prey. If you are grappling a creature at the start of your turn, you can use your swift action to deal bludgeoning damage equal to 1d6 + your Strength modifier to the creature you are grappling. If you and the creature you are grappling or attempting to grapple are both at least waist deep in water, you have a +2 size bonus to the combat maneuver check made to grapple your target and prevent it from escaping.

Eagle: You are constantly aware of your surroundings, even in the thick of combat. You cannot be surprised. When you are hit by an attack that deals extra damage, you can use your immediate action to reduce the attack's extra damage

by 1d10 + your Dexterity modifier (minimum of 0). If you reduce the extra damage to 0, you ignore any other effect that the extra damage normally causes.

Frog: You feel equally at home fighting in water as you do on dry land. You can hold your breath for 15 minutes, and you deal damage normally when making a melee weapon attack while underwater.

Jaguar: Your predatory instincts tell you when and how to pounce on a wounded foe. When a creature you can see within reach that is at its hit point maximum gets hit by an attack that reduces its hit points below its hit point maximum, you can use your immediate action to make a melee attack against that creature. When you do so, you have a +2 divine bonus on your melee attack roll.

Monkey: Celebration rejuvenates you more than rest. When you sleep for the night, if you or another creature within 60 feet of you that you can see and hear succeeds on a DC 15 Perform (any) check, you regain all hit points and ability damage after completing your rest for the night. If the check fails, you regain hit points and ability damage as you normally would after finishing a night's rest. No more than one creature can attempt the Perform (any) check over the course of the same night.

Serpent: You are equally comfortable standing upright or lying flat on your belly. You can move normally while crawling. In addition, you can drop prone or stand up from being prone as a free action.

Feats Craft Wondrous Item; **Spells** *beast shape II*;
  Price 8,000 gp

DEATH WHISTLE

Aura faint evocation; **CL** 3rd; **Slot** —; **Price** 7,200 gp; **Weight** —

This item can be used 3 times per day. You can use a standard action to emit a horrific sound resembling hundreds of terrified voices screaming in unison in a 20-foot cone that is audible 400 feet away. Each humanoid in the cone must succeed on a DC 12 Will saving throw or take 2d6 sonic damage and become frightened for one minute. On a successful Will saving throw, the creature is not frightened, and becomes immune to the effects of this *death whistle* for 24 hours. Deafened creatures and creatures immune to being frightened take no sonic damage and are not frightened. A creature that fails its Will saving throw can repeat it at the end of each of its turns, ending the frightened effect on itself on a success.

Feats Craft Wondrous Item; **Spells** *cause fear, sound burst*;
  Price 3,600 gp

EAGLE HEADDRESS

Aura faint transmutation; **CL** 7th; **Slot** headband;
  Price 9,000 gp; **Weight** 1 lb.

Eagle feathers adorn the sides and top of this headwear, while a long, slender beak covers the wearer's forehead. While wearing this headdress, you have a +2 enhancement bonus on Perception checks that rely on sight. You can also use a standard action to transform into an eagle, as *beast shape II* once per day.

Feats Craft Wondrous Item; **Spells** *beast shape II*;
  Price 4,500 gp

FEATHER SHIELD

Aura moderate conjuration; **CL** 10th; **Slot** —; **Price** 12,157 gp;
  Weight 10 lbs.

This *+2 heavy wooden shield* is made from tightly packed layers of eagle, falcon, or condor feathers bonded together with pine resin. While holding this shield, you can speak its command word as a move action to cause it to sprout wings and talons for one minute. As a swift action, you can direct the talons to make one of the following melee weapon attacks with the wielder's base attack bonus.

Slash: 2d6 slashing damage.

Grab: The target is grappled. While grappled, you can use your swift action on subsequent turns to release the target or to move the shield and the creature it is grappling up to 20 feet. The shield can fly or move along the ground. If you release the grappled creature while airborne, the creature takes 1d6 fall damage for every 10 feet it falls, up to a maximum of 20d6. When you choose to move the creature the shield is grappling, you must take off the shield as a move action, which causes you to lose the shield's bonus to AC. When the grapple ends, the shield returns to your hand at the end of your next turn.

The *feather shield* can be used 3 times per day.

Feats Craft Magic Arms and Armor; **Spells** *summon nature's ally IV*; **Cost** 6,157 gp

HELM OF THE EBON SERPENT

Aura faint transmutation; **CL** 5th; **Slot** head; **Price** 18,000 gp;
  Weight 1 lb.

Fashioned in the shape of lashing serpent's head, this light helm is crafted from lacquered wicker covered in black snakeskin. The wearer's face is framed by a gaping mouth with fangs in each corner. A crest of ebony-colored feathers adorns the top and runs down the neck.

While wearing the helm, you can use a standard action to spit venom at a creature within 15 feet of you as a ranged attack dealing 4d6 acid damage, and the target must make a successful DC 15 Fortitude saving throw or be blinded and poisoned with black adder venom. At the end of each of its turns, the target can attempt another saving throw. If the saving throw succeeds, the target is no longer blinded. The *helm of the ebon serpent* can be used 3 times per day.

Feats Craft Wondrous Item; **Spells** *beast shape I*; **Price** 9,000 gp

JAGUAR CLOAK

Aura moderate transmutation; **CL** 11th; **Slot** shoulder;
  Price 60,000 gp; **Weight** 8 lbs.

Stitched together from the pelts of Tehuatl's largest cat, this spotted garment also serves as a status symbol among the Aztli nobility. While wearing it, you gain the following benefits:

• You have a climb speed equal to your base move speed.
• You have a +8 racial bonus on Stealth checks made to hide while in grassland, forest, or swamp terrain.
• When you make a charge, you can make a full attack.

Feats Craft Wondrous Item; **Spells** *beast shape III*;
  Price 30,000 gp

LUCKY FINGERS

Aura faint divination; **CL** 3rd; **Slot** —; **Price** 1,200 gp;
  Weight —

These hideous trinkets appear to be a collection of 1d4 dried human finger bones held together only by hard, dry cartilage. They are usually found tied in a bundle hanging from a leather cord or stuffed in a pouch. You may use a swift action to snap a bone in two, which gives you a +2 luck bonus on your next ability check, saving throw, or attack roll made before the end of your next turn. When snapped, the magic in that digit is released, rendering it worthless. This trinket is crafted with 4 fingers.

Feats Craft Wondrous Item; **Spells** *guidance*; **Price** 600 gp

MACUAHUITL OF REVEALING

Aura moderate abjuration; **CL** 10th; **Slot** —; **Price** 32,310 gp;
  Weight 2 lbs.

When you hit a shapechanger with this *+2 macuahuitl*, the shapechanger takes an extra 3d6 damage, and it must succeed on a DC 15 Constitution check or revert to its original form. The shapechanger cannot assume a different form for one minute after it fails its Constitution check. Legends claim the hero-gods used these weapons to unmask the emperor's serpent-advisors.

Feats Craft Magical Arms and Armor; **Spells** *true form*;
  Price 16,310 gp

Macuahuitl of Quiahuitl

Aura moderate abjuration; **CL** 10th; **Slot** —; **Price** 4,310 gp;
  Weight 2 lbs.

This +1 macuahuitl is carved from heavily lacquered dark wood and set with rows of gleaming obsidian teeth. The flats of the club bear engravings of a serpent coiled around a cornstalk set above a flooded plain. A tightly wrapped snakeskin covers a long wooden handle tipped with a collection of six heron feathers dyed orange and blue that dangle from a woven string.

As a swift action, the weapon deals 1d4 cold damage to you by siphoning off a portion of your lifeforce as a sacrifice to Quiahuitl. When you do so, the weapon deals an extra 1d6 electricity damage until the end of your turn. You do not deal extra damage if you do not take any cold damage.

Feats Craft Magical Arms and Armor; **Spells** *call lightning* or *lightning bolt*; **Price** 2,310 gp

Mask of Smoke and Mirrors

Aura faint transmutation; **CL** 9th; **Slot** head; **Price** 30,000 gp;
  Weight 1 lb.

This decorative turquoise mask is most commonly associated with the worshippers and priests of Itztliteotl. Deerskin straps attached to the sides of the mask keep it securely fastened around your head while completely covering your face. While wearing this mask, you can see normally in lightly obscured and heavily obscured areas caused by fog, mist, or smoke to a distance of 120 feet. When you are in area containing fog, mist, or smoke, you can use your swift action to teleport up to 30 feet to an unoccupied space you can see within the fog, mist, or smoke.

Feats Craft Wondrous Item; **Spells** *darkvision, dimension door*; **Price** 15,000 gp

Mask of Quiahuitl

Aura faint transmutation; **CL** 3rd; **Slot** head; **Price** 9,000 gp;
  Weight 1 lb.

This stylized mask of lacquered ebon wood has long fangs and wide eyehole carvings that make the wearer appear to have oversized bulging eyeballs. The mask is topped with an elaborate headdress made from heron feathers. While wearing the mask, you can see through a lightly or heavily obscured area caused by foul weather such as fog, rain, sleet, wind, and other forms of precipitation.

As a standard action, you can use the mask to gaze at a creature you can see within 30 feet. The target of your gaze must succeed on a DC 12 Will saving throw. On a failed saving throw, the creature is either frightened for one minute or affected by a *command* spell (your choice). The *mask of Quiahuitl*'s gaze can be used 3 times a day.

Feats Craft Wondrous Item; **Spells** *command, darkvision*;
  Price 4,500 gp

Obsidian Dagger

Aura moderate abjuration; **CL** 10th; **Slot** —; **Price** 55,301 gp;
  Weight 1 lb.

Carved from a single shard of razor-sharp obsidian, this +1 dagger differs from the ceremonial daggers often used in sacrificial rites. Its blade fits into a cedarwood handle carved into the likeness of a pouncing jaguar. When you attack an animal, fey, humanoid, or magical beast and roll a 20 on the attack roll, you rip open a vicious gash. Then roll another d20. If you roll a 20, the blade pierces the target's heart, dealing an extra 10d6 piercing damage, and forces the creature to succeed on a DC 15 Constitution check or fall unconscious. The target then loses 3d6 hit points at the start of each of its turns. Receiving magical healing is the only way to close the wound. (If you determine the target has no heart or if the target is immune to piercing damage, the creature does not take the extra piercing damage, and it cannot fall unconscious, though it still loses 3d6 hit points at the start of each of its turns.) If you roll any number other than a 20, the target takes 2d6 bleed damage at the start of each of its turns from the extreme

blood loss, but suffers no other ill effects. If you tear open another gash after the first, the damage dealt by the gash increases by 2d6.

Feats Craft Magical Arms and Armor; **Spells** *keen edge*;
  Price 27,801 gp

Pamitl of Combat Coordination

Aura faint divination; **CL** 4th; **Slot** body; **Price** 2,400 gp;
  Weight 3 lbs.

Brightly colored feathers adorn the top of this lightweight wooden pole that is strapped to your back. While you carry the pamitl in this manner, you can use an immediate action when you roll initiative to cause its feathers to instantly shift places. Each companion within 60 feet who can see you and has not yet taken a turn in combat may swap their place in the initiative order with another affected companion for the remainder of the combat. For example, if your companions rolled a 17, 13, and 10 on their initiative checks and have not yet taken a turn in combat, you can use this feature to allow them to rearrange which of them acts on initiative count 17, initiative count 13, and initiative count 10. A creature cannot take a turn on more than one initiative count or take more than one turn in a round. The pamitl can be used 1 time per day. A character must wear this item continuously for 24 hours before they can activate this ability.

Feats Craft Wondrous Item; **Spells** *anticipate peril, unprepared combatant*; **Price** 1,200 gp

Pumpkin Seed

Aura faint divination; **CL** 7th; **Slot** —; **Price** 2,800 gp;
  Weight —

You can use a standard action to eat a pumpkin seed. When you do so, your eyes emit a faint, yellowish glow shedding dim light in a 20-foot cone that you can aim as a free action on your turn for 10 minutes. An undead or evil outsider that moves into the cone or starts its turn within the cone must succeed on a DC 16 Will saving throw or take 2d6 damage. On a successful Will saving throw, the undead or evil outsider takes half as much damage. In addition, you can use your action to end the faint, yellowish glow and instead cause your eyes to emit a blinding flash of pure light in a 20-foot cone that lasts until the end of your turn and the seed's effects end. Each creature within the cone must succeed on a DC 16 Fortitude saving throw or be blinded. Undead and evil outsiders have a -4 penalty on their Fortitude saving throw against being blinded. At the end of each of its turns, a creature blinded by the preceding effect can make another Fortitude saving throw. On a success, the creature is no longer blinded.

Feats Craft Wondrous Item; **Spells** *holy smite*; **Price** 1,400 gp

Ring of Iron

Aura moderate abjuration; **CL** 11th; **Slot** ring; **Price** 32,000 gp;
  Weight —

The Firebrand dwarves originally forged these expertly crafted iron rings as tokens of appreciation for trusted allies and loyal friends, yet over time they came to realize the rings' usefulness outweighed their ceremonial purpose. While wearing this ring, you have resist 10 fire and resist 10 electricity. In addition, items on your person made from ferrous metals and their alloys are immune to rust caused by natural forces. You also have a +2 competence bonus on Appraise checks made to estimate the value of an object containing an iron component.

Feats Forge Ring; **Spells** *resist energy*; **Cost** 16,000 gp

Ring of Pursuing

Aura moderate divination; **CL** 7th; **Slot** ring; **Price** 42,000 gp;
  Weight —

Made from the vertebra of a large, predatory animal, this undecorated bone ring appears more fearsome when worn as a nose ring rather than wrapped around a finger. While wearing this ring, you can use a standard action to speak its command word. When you do so, choose a creature that you can see within 30 feet. For the next minute, you know the target's exact location if it is in contact with ground contiguous to the same ground as you in the same plane of existence. If you know the target's exact location, the target must succeed on a DC 16 Will saving throw when it attempts to move more than 30 feet away from you. On a failed Will saving throw, the target becomes entangled and anchored until the beginning of its next turn. You cannot select a new target until the current target drops to 0 hit points or the allotted minute expires, whichever happens first.

Feats Forge Ring; **Spells** *entangle, locate creature*; **Cost** 21,000 gp

SANDALS OF THE MITOTE

Aura faint divination; **CL** 7th; **Slot** feet; **Price** 20,000 gp; **Weight** 1 lb.

These durable sandals are made from maguey fibers and have woven fabric straps that fasten the shoes to your feet. While you wear these sandals, you have a +2 enhancement bonus on Perform (dance) checks. In addition, you can move through a hostile creature's space regardless of its size, though you treat the space as difficult terrain, and you cannot willingly end your move in its space. If your movement provokes an attack of opportunity, make a Perform (dance) check against the creature's attack roll as an immediate action. If your result is greater than the attacking creature's attack roll, that creature cannot make an attack of opportunity against you until the start of your next turn and the attack automatically misses.

Feats Craft Wondrous Item; **Spells** *jester's jaunt*; **Price** 10,000 gp

SEAL OF MIQUITO

Aura strong conjuration; **CL** 15th; **Slot** —; **Price** 60,000 gp; **Weight** 3 lbs.

This strange stone vessel is circular shaped, about six inches in diameter and three inches tall. The sides bear thousands of ancient runes while a grinning skull is carved into the top. The seal separates into two pieces and feels unusually light (it is hollow). As a standard action, the seal's outsider owner can force the soul of any humanoid that it can see within 100 feet of it to depart its body and enter the seal. The target resists their soul being taken with a successful DC 20 Will saving throw, which also prevents the owner from trying to take the target's soul for 24 hours. On a failed saving throw, the target's soul leaves the body and is trapped within the seal. Once used in this way, the seal cannot be used again for seven days.

The target's body falls into a catatonic state. If the seal is destroyed and the target's body is less than 100 feet away from the seal and is still alive, the soul returns to the body and the target regains consciousness. Otherwise, the target dies. The seal cannot contain more than one soul at any time. If another soul already occupies the seal, the attempt to possess another soul automatically fails. The owner can free a trapped soul from the seal as a standard action. A good outsider uses this magic item to bring a worthy soul to its just rewards in the afterlife. Evil outsiders use the seal to sacrifice unwilling souls to their fiendish masters or a malevolent deity.

Feats Craft Wondrous Item; **Spells** *trap the soul*; **Price** 30,000 gp

SERPENT SHIELD

Aura faint abjuration; **CL** 3rd; **Slot** —; **Price** 1,225 gp; **Weight** 3 lbs.

This small, round *+1 light wooden shield* is crafted from a wicker and wood frame covered with lacquer and serpent's skin and adorned with feathers and various patterns of color to denote the status of whoever carries it. You gain a +2 circumstance bonus to Intimidate checks while wearing this shield.

Feats Craft Magical Arms and Armor; **Spells** —; **Price** 725 gp

STAFF OF WILDERNESS EXPLORATION

Aura moderate divination; **CL** 11th; **Slot** —; **Price** 22,000 gp; **Weight** 5 lbs.

This staff has the following abilities and actions:

• *Exploration.* By spending one charge, your speed increases by 10 feet and you always sense the direction of true north while holding the staff for 24 hours. In addition, you can use a full-round action to touch one end of the staff to the ground and speak its command word. For the next minute, you know the direction of the nearest natural hazard, such as quicksand or a volcano, within 500 feet, but not its distance from you.
  • *detect disease* (1 charge)
  • *detect poison* (0 charges)
  • *find the path* (6 charges)
  • *freedom of movement* (4 charges)
  • *water walk* (3 charges)

Feats Craft Staff; **Spells** *detect disease, detect poison, find the path, freedom of movement, water walk*; **Price** 11,000 gp

STONE OF STUNNING

Aura strong enchantment; **CL** 15th; **Slot** —; **Price** 5,000 gp; **Weight** —

Made from hard rubber, these spherical sling stones are designed to debilitate rather than kill an enemy. When you hit a creature with the stone, the stone deals 1 bludgeoning damage instead of normal damage. The target must succeed on a DC 22 Fortitude saving throw or be stunned. At the end of each of its turns, a creature stunned by the stone may make another Fortitude saving throw. On a success, the creature is no longer stunned.

Once a stone deals damage to a creature, it becomes a nonmagical stone. Other types of magic ammunition of this kind exist, such as rubber-tipped *arrows of stunning* or *bolts of stunning*, though stones are the most common variety.

Feats Craft Magical Arms and Armor; **Spells** *power word stun*; **Price** 2,500 gp

STORYBOOK CODEX

Aura strong universal; **CL** 20th; **Slot** —; **Price** 100,000 gp; **Weight** 5 lbs.

This codex contains six fables presented in a pictorial format on the book's amate pages. If you spend 48 hours over a period of six or more days studying and interpreting the book's artistic content, you must then succeed on a DC 15 Intelligence check to understand the meaning of each of the six tales within the storybook. (You make a separate Intelligence check for each of the six stories, and you can study and interpret the codex's meaning only once in your lifetime.) The storybook then loses its magic, but regains it in one year. If you fail your Intelligence check on a particular story, you learn nothing from that story and gain no benefits from its wisdom. With a successful Intelligence check, you gain the benefits from the story corresponding to your successful Intelligence check as presented below:

The Beggar and the Priest: This cautionary tale of greed and ambition teaches you to better understand the motives of others. You gain a +4 inherent bonus to Sense Motive checks.

The Crocodile Whisperer: On the banks of a murky river, one member of a hunting party dips his toes into the water to lure out a hungry crocodile who then bites off his foot while his companions subdue the mighty reptile. Unlike the hapless hunter in this tale, when an ethereal, invisible, disguised, or hidden creature makes a melee attack against you, you are not caught flat-footed.

The Dance of Death: A mischievous host tricks his guests into dancing themselves to exhaustion to irresistibly addictive music. Refusing to follow the same fate, you can remove the fatigued condition or reduce the exhausted condition to fatigued once per day as a standard action.

The Sacrifice of Nauhuatzal: This story extols the virtues of sacrificing yourself to save countless other lives. Once per day, you can use a standard action to touch a willing creature. When you do so, the creature touched regains hit points equal to the amount it would gain from a paladin's lay on hands, with effective level equal to your Hit Dice. You, in turn, take an amount of damage equal to half the hit points the target creature regained.

The Skeleton with a Heart: This macabre fable ultimately speaks to the honorable notion of achieving wealth and fame through integrity and hard work. In this story, a cunning skeleton offers to handsomely reward anyone who could pull his still-beating heart out of his chest. Although the dare was a ruse in the grim tale, you acquire a better understanding about how to precisely manipulate objects with your hands and use precision tools. You gain a +4 inherent bonus to Sleight of Hand checks.

The Temptation of Cuatepetli: After drinking too much pulque, a noble and respected family patriarch disgraces himself and his family when he commits an unforgiveable transgression. To help prevent you from following in Cuatepetli's footsteps, you gain a +2 inherent bonus to saves against poison.

Feats Craft Wondrous Item; **Spells** *wish*; **Price** 50,000 gp

TANGLED GOURD

Aura faint transmutation; **CL** 1st; **Slot** —; **Price** 150 gp;
Weight 1 lb.

This roughly spherical green, orange, or bright yellow gourd is three inches in diameter and weighs one pound. You can use a standard action to throw the gourd up to 40 feet. The gourd rips apart on impact and fills the area with fibrous vines for one minute. Each creature within a 10-foot radius of where the gourd lands must succeed on a DC 12 Reflex saving throw or be entangled by the vines. The affected area becomes difficult terrain. A creature that enters the affected area for the first time or an unentangled creature that starts its turn in the affected area must succeed on a DC 12 Reflex saving throw to avoid being entangled. A creature already entangled by the vines at the start of its turn takes 2d6 bludgeoning damage. A creature restrained by the vines can use a standard action to free itself. To do so, it must succeed on a DC 12 Strength or Escape Artist check. When the vines disappear after one minute, all entangled creatures are freed, and the affected area reverts to whatever terrain it was before the vines appeared.

Feats Craft Wondrous Item; **Spells** *entangle*; **Price** 75 gp

TILMAHTLI OF FLOWERS

Aura faint transmutation; **CL** 3rd; **Slot** shoulders; **Price** 1,000 gp; **Weight** 1 lb.

This white linen cloak features red, yellow, and blue flower petals stitched onto the fabric. While you wear this garment with the hood up, the flowers release a subtle yet perceivable sweet aroma in a 20-foot radius that animals and humanoids find pleasurable and soothing. You have a +2 alchemical on your Bluff, Diplomacy, and Intimidate checks whenever you interact with an animal or humanoid within 20 feet of you. Each animal or humanoid within 20 feet of you has a -2 penalty on its saving throws against being charmed by you or magically put to sleep by you. While you emit the floral aura, you have a -2 penalty on Stealth checks made to hide, while Perception checks relying on smell to notice you have a +2 alchemical bonus. Creatures with the Scent special ability automatically succeed on their Perception checks to notice you. Pulling the hood up or down requires a move action. The aroma dissipates at the end of your next turn when you pull the hood down.

Feats Craft Wondrous Item; **Spells** *scent trail*; **Price** 500 gp

TILMAHTLI OF THE OWL

Aura moderate illusion; **CL** 5th; **Slot** shoulders; **Price** 6,000 gp; Weight 1 lb.

This dark linen cloak bears the image of an owl with outstretched wings stitched onto the fabric. While wearing it, you can use a standard action to grip the edges of the cloak with both hands and raise and lower them to simulate an owl in flight. When you do so in an area of bright light or dim light, you cast an ominous shadow in a 20-foot cone. Each creature within the cone must succeed on a DC 14 Will saving throw or take 5d6 damage and be haunted by an intangible, malevolent owl spirit that has no physical form. Mindless creatures and creatures with animal intelligence are not affected. On a successful Will saving throw, the creature takes half damage and is not haunted.

A haunted creature senses the owl spirit's presence hovering over its head even though nothing is actually there. Each time the haunted creature takes damage from a source other than this effect, it takes an extra 1d6 damage and it cannot take attacks of opportunity until the end of its next turn. At the end of each of its turns, a haunted creature can make another Will saving throw.

(A haunted creature who took damage since the end of its last turn has a -2 penalty on this saving throw.) On a successful Will saving throw, the creature is no longer haunted. You can use the tilmahtli again in this way once per day.

Feats Craft Wondrous Item; **Spells** *phantasmal reminder*; **Price** 3,000 gp

TLATCHLI BALL

Aura moderate transmutation; **CL** 9th; **Slot** —; **Price** 54,000 gp; **Weight** 9 lbs.

This solid, rubber ball weighs nine pounds and has black and red swirling patterns painted on it. You can use a standard action to speak the ball's command word. When you do so, the ball flies out of your hand and travels in a line that is five feet wide and 120 feet long. When the ball reaches the end of the line, it falls harmlessly to the ground. You can use your swift action to cause the ball to instantly return to your hand. Each creature in that line must succeed on a DC 12 Reflec saving throw or take 5d6 bludgeoning damage and get knocked prone. A creature who succeeds on its Reflex saving throw takes half as much damage and is not knocked prone. This ball can be used 3 times per day.

Feats Craft Wondrous Item; **Spells** *telekinesis*; **Price** 27,000 gp

TURQUOISE NACOCHTLI

Aura faint conjuration; **CL** 3rd; **Slot** —; **Price** 400 gp; **Weight** —

Originally given to esteemed midwives, these ornate earplugs magically adjust to painlessly elongate and then fit inside your earlobes. While you wear them, you have a +2 competence bonus on Heal checks.

Feats Craft Wondrous Item; **Spells** *cure light wounds*; **Price** 200 gp

WAR PAINT

Aura moderate varies; **CL** 9th; **Slot** —; **Price** 9,000 gp; **Weight** —

Typically stored in clay jars two inches in diameter, each container holds 1d3 applications of viscous pigments made from dyes and other colorful components. Each jar contains one color of paint, and its contents weigh half a pound. As a standard action, one dose of war paint can be rubbed onto the skin. The pigment covers roughly six square inches of skin. A creature can wear no more than three different colors of paint at a time, and you cannot simultaneously apply the effects of more than one color of *war paint* to the same weapon. Any attempt to apply more than three colors of war paint fails. Each application of paint lasts for 10 minutes regardless of color. The *war paint*'s color determines its effects. When crafted each container contains 3 applications of the same color.

Black: Necromantic energy fills your soul. You can use a swift action on each of your turns to condemn each creature other than an undead or construct that can see or hear you within 30 feet. Each targeted creature must succeed on a DC 17 Will saving throw or take 1d8 + 9 negative energy damage. On a successful Will saving throw, the target takes half as much damage and is immune to this *war paint*'s effects for 24 hours.

Blue: A frigid chill courses through your body. While your wear this war paint, you can use a swift action to cause one weapon you are holding to coat itself in frost until the beginning of your next turn. The icy coating is harmless to you and the weapon. When you hit with an attack using the frosty weapon, it deals an extra 1d6 cold damage.

Green: Nothing can hold you back. You cannot be entangled or paralyzed. You can use five feet of your movement to automatically escape a grapple.

Orange: You never back down and thrive when the odds are stacked against you. You are immune to fear. If two or more hostile creature are within five feet of you at the start of your turn, you may use your swift action to make a melee attack against one of the hostile creatures if it is within reach.

Purple: You are a whirlwind in combat. When a creature you can see within reach takes damage from a melee attack during another creature's turn, you can use an attack of opportunity to make a melee attack against the creature that took the damage.

Red: Warmth radiates through your skin. While you wear this war paint, you can use a swift action to cause one weapon you are holding to glow red-hot until the beginning of your next turn. The heat is harmless to you and the weapon. When you hit with an attack using the fiery weapon, it deals an extra 1d6 fire damage.

White: Sacred forces guide your actions. You can use a swift action on each of your turns to damage each undead that can see or hear you within 30 feet. Each fiend or undead must succeed on a DC 17 Will saving throw or take 1d8 + 9 positive energy damage. On a successful Will saving throw, the undead takes half as much damage and is immune to this war paint's effects for 24 hours.

Yellow: Electrical energy surges within you. While you wear this war paint, you can use a swift action to cause one weapon you are holding to crackle with electrical energy until the beginning of your next turn. The electricity is harmless to you and the weapon. When you hit with an attack using the charged weapon, it deals an extra 1d6 electricity damage.

Feats Craft Wondrous Item; **Spells** *mass inflict light wounds* (black), *ice storm* (blue), *freedom of movement* (green), *heroism* (orange), *true strike* (purple), *flame strike* (red), *mass cure light wounds* (white), *lightning bolt* (yellow); **Price** 4,500 gp

XTABENTUN

Aura faint conjuration; **CL** 11th; **Slot** —; **Price** 16,000 gp; **Weight** —

This fermented beverage made from honey, tree bark, and corn allows the drinker to momentarily defy reality. When found, a vial contains 1d3 + 1 one-ounce doses of the prized liqueur. You can use a standard action to drink a dose. The effects last for one minute. The instant you swallow it, you experience a sense of euphoria. You gain 10 temporary hit points and become immune to fear. In addition, you can use your immediate action to enter a transcendental state until the end of your next turn when *xtabentun*'s effects suddenly end. When you use the magical elixir in this way, you become ethereal. Any harmful abilities or magical effects that would affect you while you are in the transcendental state do not take effect until the liqueur's magic wears off. If you can counteract the harmful ability or magical effect in the interim, you negate the harmful ability or magical effect in its entirety. This item is crafted with 4 doses.

Feats Craft Wondrous Item; **Spells** *ether step*; **Price** 8,000 gp